KU-415-292

Contents

A Thief in the Night

And Other Adventures of the Septimus Society

Stephen
Wade

A3 443 553 1

OLDHAM METRO
LIBRARY SERVICE

A34435531

Bertrams	05/09/2014
CRI	£7.99
OLD	

First published 2014

The Mystery Press is an imprint of The History Press
The Mill, Brimscombe Port
Stroud, Gloucestershire, GL5 2QG
www.thehistorypress.co.uk

© Stephen Wade, 2014

The right of Stephen Wade to be identified as the Author
of this work has been asserted in accordance with the
Copyright, Designs and Patents Act 1988.

All rights reserved. No part of this book may be reprinted
or reproduced or utilised in any form or by any electronic,
mechanical or other means, now known or hereafter invented,
including photocopying and recording, or in any information
storage or retrieval system, without the permission in writing
from the Publishers.

British Library Cataloguing in Publication Data.
A catalogue record for this book is available from the British Library.

ISBN 978 0 7509 5628 4

Typesetting and origination by The History Press
Printed in Great Britain

The Septimus Society

Lord George Lenham-Cawde

Lord George, as the tall aristocrat is known, has a special interest in danger and the risk taken in the pursuit of villains. This stems from his service in India and in Egypt, in the Royal Horse Guards (The Blues). He has also spent some time in espionage, doing his part in the Great Game against Russia. He has an old enemy in Colonel Velkov, who later ran a spy ring in Paris. Lord George has a penchant for the turf and for acquiring a voluminous knowledge of crime in the city.

Professor Harry Lacey PhD, Cambridge

Harry Lacey is an eminent literary critic of Jesus College, Cambridge. He is a specialist in English poetry of the Elizabethan period. He has been allotted the task of keeping the Septimus Society records, and tends to work with Lord George on most cases.

When his thoughts are not on sonnets, they are on high-class dining and solid English cuisine. He is a close friend of Arthur Sullivan, the composer.

Maria de Bellezza

Maria is an Italian society lady, with a cultural circle which welcomes foreign writers and artists to London. Her forte is in diplomacy and she tends to be assigned to special detective services for such matters as assassination and terrorism threats. But her principal role is that of information-gatherer, and she makes it her business to meet anyone who is anyone in London. At her parties, she uses the occasions for gathering useful information for her contacts in Special Branch.

Jemmy Smythe

Smythe is a gentleman's gentleman at the Septimus Society in Piccadilly, where members spend most of their time. His experience as an ex-jockey and bookie proves useful for many of the Society's cases.

Detective Inspector Edward Carney

Eddie is the one professional in the Septimus Society, having gone through the ranks in the Metropolitan

Police. He has had experience of all varieties of city policing, and knows the range of scams and frauds in the white collar crime categories. He is well known across the City and the East End, and he works closely with the Thames River Police at Wapping, as earlier in his career he was with them. He met Lord George and Harry Lacey at a retirement celebration for his Commissioner in 1883, and leapt at the chance to join the Society.

Cara Cabrelli

The newest member of the Septimus Society, Cara is an actress and singer, very much in demand in the bustling, frenetic world of London theatre. Just twenty-two, she has a mind of her own, is strong-willed and not at all afraid of danger. In fact, she has a sense of adventure and welcomes the challenge a spot of trouble can bring.

Joe Sidebottom (aka Aubrey Leo Antoine)

Sensational novelist Leo (as he is known to his friends) has a keen interest in amateur criminology, and, of course, is always hunting for potential plots as he works with the Septimus Society on their cases. Under the cheery façade and the rattle of his talk there is the acute, incisive mind of an amateur sleuth. He is forty, but behaves like a Regency playboy, and one of the great thrills of his life was being elected a member of the Septimus Society. A considerable city celebrity (the author of *Midnight Danger*, a Balkan mystery), his readers would expect to see him rubbing shoulders with the aristocracy and attending hunt balls.

His family are brewers from Leeds, and Leo's battle to erase his Tyke vowels has been won by his developing a cut-glass accent. His father became extremely rich and Leo inherited a mansion in one of the most desirable addresses in London.

Leo has a weakness for women and romantic adventures, and tends to be assigned to cases involving subtle information-gathering at wealthy, grand parties.

The Society Welcomes Maria

London, 1890

It all began in the Oriental Hotel on the edge of Hyde Park, when Maria de Bellezza, the honoured guest invited to join the men and Cara at the table for dinner, started talking about her penchant for murder. 'I find a clean, tidy murder more satisfying than the greatest watercolour or a portrait by Rembrandt. There's something artistic and of the highest order about such a feat.'

She had said this after Harry Lacey, Professor of English, had threatened to become extremely boring on the subject of John Donne's *Holy Sonnets*. His opening words had made Lord George Lenham-Cawde splutter as he almost choked on his Chablis. 'Please, Harry, no more poetry!'

They had been meeting for dinner on the first Friday of every month for a few years now, and enjoyed the gentle teasing and tales of scrapes and adventures in pursuit of either criminals or of sheer pleasure in the city.

Maria was a true European and took a wider, more tolerant view of Harry's literary harmlessness, but her words on murder provoked Harry to respond, with his usual boyish glee, 'I say, why don't we start a murder club?' He looked around the table of old friends, veterans of student parties and high society art exhibitions. Then he proceeded to address his words to each in turn: 'You, George, are preoccupied with the horrific tales of the *Newgate Calendar*; you, Maria dear, have even dined with several notorious villains; Smythe, you have spent half your life alongside the schemers and fraudsters of the turf; Eddie, you, as mere duty, actually spend your time among killers in your professional capacity at the Yard; and as for you, Leo, why, you make up the most ridiculous, melodramatic plots ever perpetrated in literature, and therefore it is high time you were faced with real, living rogues.' Everyone laughed at this, except that is for a young lady at the end of the table. 'My dear Professor, why omit my good self? Is it simply because I am young?'

Harry sipped his wine and then said, beaming with pleasure, 'We must welcome Cara Cabrelli, everyone … the newest recruit to our dining circle. Cara, my dear young lady, you are a thespian. No villain stalks the boards! Of course, given the rather questionable status of actresses in our lamentably blinkered society, it is only fitting that you should engage in the respectable pursuit of detection. But as I say, surely the theatre has no rogues?'

'Hah!' Cara snorted. 'Harry, you may be very clever, knowing Latin and all kinds of long words, but you are absolutely wrong in this instance. Why, the theatre is riddled with criminals, like worms in a smelly cheese!'

Cara continued, 'As to the disgusting opinion that we ladies of the stage are but one step away from ... well, ladies of the night ... that is something a civilized society should leave behind!'

Again there was general laughter. Cara went on, 'In fact, in criminal matters, a member of the cast in my last production heartlessly killed a man because he was overlooked for a role that went to his victim. Yes, and he was a man who had courted me, by the way, a man I esteemed greatly until that dreadful day.'

'What, did you actually *see* the murder my dear?' Lord George asked.

'Well no, but it was reported graphically by Carrington Kleiderman, the tenor.'

'Oh well, if he saw it then it must be true!' Smythe said, teasingly. 'But I have to say, speaking as a man who has seen skulduggery on the turf in its most extreme form, that murder is not a matter for fun or recreation.' The former jockey was a thin man, very lightly built, having scarcely added a pound to his frame since riding his last horse in 1887, three years previously. 'There is a fashion these days for treating the crime of homicide in a way which is no more realistic and convincing than the worst fantasies of a certain class of popular novelist ... hey Leo?'

There was general amusement at this tease, and Leo, taking it well, joined in the laughter at his own expense. 'Now, Jemmy, you know very well that I apply myself to assiduous research for my novels. People think I simply dash them off with the same haste as I would make a slice of toast. But I sweat and labour over every page like a coal miner!'

'And you should know about that, as you have a number of such men in your family history I'm sure!' Maria cajoled him. 'And your Pa was ever such a manual worker ... with his millions made from other poor workers in his breweries!'

'Well there are worse trades than brewing. He merely gave the working man what he craved when he had laboured by the sweat of his brow all day. If he made a guinea or two out of it, then so what?'

'A guinea or two! He lives in the same neighbourhood as two Americans who are filthy rich from industry in the cowboy land!' Maria said, unable to resist baiting him.

As the laughter subsided, Detective Inspector Edward Carney stepped in. 'Very well, let us play the sleuth. At the Yard we have people coming forward all the time offering to solve crimes for us. It's a national passion, involving vicars' wives and retired office clerks, dowagers and dairymen. But you will have to prove yourselves capable and nimble in the wits. Shall you try to solve a case ... one I shall present to you now, over brandy and cigars?'

'Why yes, and the ladies will remain with us ... none of that division of the sexes in *our* club!' declared George.

'Very well, then here we go. It reads like such a simple, uncomplicated statement of a killing: York Assizes, 1829. Abraham Bairstan, aged sixty, was put to the bar, charged with the wilful murder of Sarah Bairstan, his wife, in the parish of Bradford. In the busy, overworked courts of the Regency, dealing with new and often puzzling crimes from the labouring classes in the fast-growing towns, it was maybe just another homely confrontation that went too far. But this is far from the truth, and the Bairstan case offers an insight into the plight of those unfortunate people who were victims of ignorance as well as of illness. In this instance it was a mental illness that played a major part in this murder – or was it?

When the turnkey brought Bairstan into the court he commented that he had not heard the prisoner say a word since he was brought to York and locked up. This was nothing new to the man's family. Mr Baron Hullock, presiding, was shocked and pressed the gaoler to explain. He asked if the man in the dock understood the spoken word, and the answer was no. He also ascertained that Bairstan appeared to have no response to any sound whatsoever, nor reacted to any movement. Poor Hullock had a real challenge to try to communicate with the man, trying his best to encourage the prisoner to make any sound at all, asking several questions but receiving no answer. When he asked in a raised voice, "Do you hear what I say to you?" Bairstan simply stared at the officer next to him.'

'The best lawyer in the country would have been confused there!' Lord George exclaimed.

Eddie continued: 'It was obviously going to be one of those trials at which many people were thinking that this silence was the best ruse if a man wanted to avoid the rope. The judge had to instruct the jury about potential fraud and the possibility that this was a tough and amoral killer with a canny wit and impressive acting skills. Legally, the point was, was the man standing there fraudulently, willfully and obstinately mute, or was his silence visited upon him "by the act and providence of God?" It was going to be a hard task, one might think, but not so: enter his sons – Henry and Joseph – and a close friend. They told a very sad story, and an astounding one, given that Bairstan managed to marry and raise a family.'

The others stared in complete fascination. 'Who spoke at the trial then?' asked Harry.

'His friend, Jeremiah Hailey, stated that he had known the prisoner for over fifty years, and that he was sure that ten years had passed since Bairstan had fallen silent. He explained that his two sons had been looking after the old man in that time. He said that while he was sane, his wife and he had lived together very comfortably. In fact, his wife had been in the habit of asking him to kneel and pray with her, almost every hour on most days. She was a holy woman. Hailey added that his friend had been capable of merely saying yes or no, and that the last time he had heard the man speak was when he had asked him if he knew him; "He said aye, but I think he did not know me".'

'Surely the man was acting?' said Cara. 'Did he have a time as an actor in his past?'

Eddie shook his head. 'No, not at all. Bairstan's two sons confirmed that their father had been silent in that ten-year period, only excepting one or two words. Henry said that since being locked up, his father had been pressed to speak and had answered something sounding like 'Be quiet ... be quiet'. Joseph confirmed that his father had been "out of his mind" for ten years.'

'Now hold on just a minute!' interrupted Lord George. 'There had been enough in him to marry and earn a living, but we must apply more curious enquiry and suggest that Abraham Bairstan had feigned being struck by a paralysis, perhaps combined with a mental illness. Surely he had observed men with that illness and copied them?'

'Not at all,' Eddie said. 'Sixty years ago the most meaningful explanation was to put his strange behavior down to God's will, so the jury found that the prisoner stood mute by the visitation of God. The question, ladies and gentlemen, is how may we have proved that he was feigning his silence and his illness?'

'The most enthralling story would have been to create a terrible shock ... force the man to speak by sheer surprise,' Leo suggested. 'Perhaps the use of a firework behind him would suffice?' There was general laughter at this.

'Typical of you, Leo,' said Harry. 'Take the story for one of your improbable plots old man!'

Leaning forward to assure herself of the full attention of the table, Cara said, 'In my experience, one should always question the improbable. Most men are charlatans, and are inept at pretence. If this Bairstan person was seen as a victim of God, and had not taken the life of his wife, and this was agreed on the testimony of sons and friends, then there is one conclusion ... his sons and friends were part of the plan. They all wanted her dead! I would far more believe *that* than a cock and bull tale about a visitation of God!'

'My dear Cara, you leave very little room for trusting that at least some human beings will have an ounce of morality,' Maria cut in. 'I think a detective has to leave a small amount of gullibility in her, so that she may learn by mistakes rather than by logic all the time.' She laughed at her own exaggeration, done entirely for effect.

'The solution is simple,' declared Leo. 'The man was driven to madness by the constant praying and therefore took his wife's life while under duress; the verdict should have been justifiable homicide, while driven insane by the woman's kneeling to pray!'

There was general laughter and the club was formally established. Detective Inspector Edward Carney said, 'Too much merriment! There is no laughter at the Yard. I therefore solemnly inaugurate the … what shall we call it?'

'Now, I am properly Septimus George, and Harry here is Septimus Harold,' said George, 'and we play chess at the Septimus Club in Piccadilly … so…'

'I therefore solemnly inaugurate the Septimus Society, a criminological brotherhood and sisterhood devoted to the investigation of those crimes which the police ignore, forget or find too baffling!' Eddie raised his glass and all seven members drank to the newly inaugurated Septimus Society.

'This is a capital idea,' said Leo. 'Why did it take us so long to see that murder is a more worthwhile topic for debate than any number of worthy causes!'

The Canlon Studios

It was an early autumn evening when Sir Simon Basson came into the library of the Septimus Society, calling out the name of Lord Lenham-Cawde. Grey-haired heads turned and voices from deep in the comfortable leather armchairs shushed and tutted at the intrusion butting into their accustomed silence like a peal of bells at early morning.

'There you are, George. By God you're a hard man to find!' Basson said, peering around the wing of Lord George Lenham-Cawde's chair, where the young peer was deep in reading the *Daily Graphic*.

'My dear Simon, how good to see you, though I was trying to concentrate on the law reports.' Lord George stood, towering above Basson, who was square and solid and of middle height, a rugger blue at college. They shook hands and Lord George pointed across to the sofa where his friend sat, enjoying scones and tea.

'You never met Harry Lacey, did you Simon? Harry, this is Sir Simon Basson, at Cambridge with me. Good scholar and a capital batsman.'

'No; pleased to meet you Harry.'

Professor Lacey was round and short, a man who enjoyed his food and drink and who was constantly ribbed and tormented by Lord George about his attempts to lose some weight.

'Glad to meet you, Sir Simon ... I've had not a word from George since he was immersed in the crime stories. All he wants to talk about today are the habitual criminals supposedly teeming in the streets.'

'Well, that's exactly right, and it's why I've come to see you. One of these blackguards has been busy taking me for a fool ... and he's succeeded.' Basson sat down, put one hand on the table to support himself and gave a deep sigh. 'I'm finding it hard to feel pleasant in the social world as I've just discovered that I've been duped, robbed absolutely. This rogue in a rather loud suit has bilked me, George, done me for almost a thousand pounds!'

Lord George ordered some brandy and sat down next to his friend, trying to console him. 'Now Simon, when you're ready, please tell me more.' George stretched his long legs out, took out a cigarette and sat back, looking intently at his friend's face. Looking back at George, Simon saw someone who was in every way composed, confident and assured. Here was a man in his late thirties, a former army man, sitting there with his short, rich black hair and that dark moustache, elegantly posed, smoking and allowing his wonderfully acute brain to set to work. He knew he had come to the right man for help. 'Come on Simon, as the great playwright said, give us a round, unvarnished tale,' he said, and Simon found the words.

'I bought a painting from this rogue ... and it's a fake, George.'

'Now how do you know the thing is a fake, my dear Simon? In all our time together as students, I knew you as a sensible, rational cove, not easily taken in...'

'Hah! Well I have been. It was at the Matchdown auction rooms I met this crook. Thought all was well, then last night – as you may know I was giving a dinner in my rooms in the very heart of Marylebone for Sparrow Warburton's new book of poems and all the aesthetic types came you know – and there I was, mine host, cheery, and trying my best to hold a conversation about Turner ... I even had that chap Grossmith there to play the piano for us ... such a droll type ... anyway I was going on about painting and showing off my new acquisition when this little chap tugs at my sleeve and, pointing to my new watercolour, he says, "Sorry to say, Sir Simon, but this picture here ... this is no F.W. Canlon I'm afraid."

'All heads turned to the picture. Then followed a lecture by this little man – some kind of lecturer I believe – as to why the pretty landscape with Lincoln Cathedral was the work of a very clever forger!'

Harry wiped his mouth clear of crumbs with a napkin, sipped the last of his tea, and said, 'Canlon ... very collectable. All his best work is Lincolnshire. Beyond my pocket though. Did he paint your place, George? George's family seat is near Horncastle, you see,' he added to Basson, in way of explanation.

'Never painted our place,' sighed Lord George. 'Go on, Simon.'

'Well I paid close on a thousand for it from this dealer ... just six weeks ago!' said Sir Simon, anger heating his every word. 'He was paid at the end of last month of course, by a bill of exchange. I came here because you have friends in the police, I hear, even in the ranks of the detectives. Word gets around about you. Is there any way you could help me, George?'

Lord George stubbed out his cigarette and turned to face his friend. 'Just a moment ... did you say that we are known for work against crime?'

'Why yes ... in the clubs and coffee houses, I think. I myself heard about you in the Turkish Baths.'

Lord George looked surprised: usually he hid his emotions very well. He was partly shocked and partly impressed. 'But we're a *secret* society, Simon ... at least I thought we were. We merely supply a need – specialist knowledge when required; if the police take no interest or meet with failure, then the Septimus Society is here. But good God, we never advertise!' He gave Harry a searching look, and the professor of literature puffed out his rosy cheeks. 'By Heaven, George, you don't think that I ...'

'All I'm saying, Harry, is that you have a tendency to speak first and think afterwards.'

Harry Lacey smiled to himself, reflecting that he was enjoying doing something entirely different to studying old books. But he pretended to be offended and pulled a face, before exclaiming, 'I'm the very soul of discretion, George ... never speak of us. It was most probably Leo; he can't keep a secret.'

Basson was growing impatient. He stood up, and for a moment George thought his friend was going to stamp his feet and have a childish tantrum, but instead he simply asked what was to be done.

George stood too, took another cigarette from his silver case, and said, 'We must go to an art auction, Simon ... but not the Matchdown. He won't show his face there again. No, he'll be at another. Then we also have the question of how he deluded you and who's the scratcher. Probably the man you met is the talker, and his scratcher's behind somewhere. What happened exactly?'

Basson told of meeting the man at the auction and then being taken in by his talk of having several paintings in his own establishment which were for sale. His argument was obvious – a private sale would avoid the auction house's cut, of course. 'He then invited me to his place, and we went to a studio where there was a man working, and pictures around the room ...'

Lord George cut in: 'Do you recall passing any significant places ... or did anything stay in the mind?'

'Yes ... yes, the sale was in Poland Street and we walked ...,' Basson frowned in concentration, '... we went through Soho Square ... then, well, it was very dark and I had, you know, taken a drink or two.'

George was putting the scene together in his mind. His friend had been talked into going with this man, then he was taken to a small room which was apparently a painter's studio. There he sold Simon the painting.

'Very well, to the art sale tomorrow! We'll try to find this rogue.' George declared.

'There's a rather grand affair at the Holborn house … at eleven.'

'Meet me there … I'll have Kate with me,' said George.

'No you won't George,' Harry said, confidently. 'Kate, as of today, is no longer with us. I meant to tell you but all you could talk about was the problem of the London criminal and the epidemic of night assaults. We lost her to a lucrative marriage.'

'Then we must recruit a woman immediately. Go home, Simon, gather your strength, and meet one of our Society there tomorrow.'

As Simon Basson left, George asked his friend, 'Where may we find a suitable actress in time for tomorrow morning?'

'Why, at The Savoy of course. I have one young lady in mind … an old friend. In fact I've had a word with her already about working with us.' Harry absent-mindedly picked up the last half scone on his plate and nibbled at it, lost in thought for a moment. 'First, I'll check my records for forgery in the art market, perhaps going back a year. I have the name Metlem in my head.'

'No. He died. Drowned in the Thames,' George said, with a triumphant smile.

'Right, so once again your memory is superior to my index cards! I'm not impressed. It's rather dismally tragic that one so young should have such petty childish victories of fact,' Harry said, adding, 'I'll look at the cards and then I'm away to the theatre, George. This is a job for Eddie. We need the police involved from the start.'

Lord George sat down and, grasping the *Daily Graphic* and stretching out his legs, settled down once more in the comfortable leather armchair. 'I'll think about how to trap our little forger,' he murmured to himself.

The door of Pentonville Prison opened, by the side of the massive entrance gates, and in the early sunshine a large, fleshy man stepped out, carrying a hessian sack in which were all the possessions he had in the world. He blinked, and screwed up his eyes, then lifted the sack over one shoulder as a warder called out behind him, 'No coming back, Tosher. We're sick of you 'ere.'

'No more than I am of you … if you ever see me again, it'll be in a coffin!'

He was tall, still quite young, in his late twenties, and had once been solid, muscled and athletic, but now he was ruined by the two years of hard labour he had endured. He had a pot belly, and the rest of him was full and fat. His face was pale and he walked slightly bent.

There was but one person waiting for him: a short, stocky, middle-aged man in expensive clothing. He wore a woollen jacket, fastened high, with a collarless check waistcoat beneath; a light green silk cravat and black striped trousers showed the world that he was well-off. A distinctive feature, standing out for anyone to see, was his glass eye and a ridge of scar tissue on the temple: evidence that he had seen some kind of accident or had been to war.

'Tosher! Very fine to see you my young friend … out in God's own light at last hey? Oh, it's been such an age!'

The younger man did not smile. He grimaced and declined to shake hands with the other.

'What's the matter? What have I done? I thought we were friends … and I have work for you, how's that? I trust they let you have drawing materials in that hell hole?'

The younger man nodded. 'Yes … some of the warders were fine with that … and the chaplain allowed me time to paint. That was the only consolation in there. Fact is, Ned, they know how to break a man.' He bent forward, a sob rising in him; he wept like a child and dropped the bag. 'Ned … Ned, I'm never going back in there! I'm going right, decent, I am, I swears it.'

'Well, Tosher, I can reassure you that the work I have for you is no more than painting! Yes … a studio and honest work with your brush. How does that sound?'

'I'll believe it when I see it Ned.'

'Well, we'll be rich, my young friend … rich. I have not been idle while you languished in that castle of pain! Though you have not been starved I perceive!'

'I ate more than my share ... you have to fight to stay on top in there.'

'So you can take it my old mate ... dog eat dog, eh?'

'Never, Ned ... never back in there. I'll die else ... I'll leave this world of sorrow.'

Ned Byrne took all this in his stride and led the way to a beer shop to give his friend some courage, in the shape of a glass of porter. His mind was a grinding machine of plans and projections; he was finding a way to bring Tosher Killane back into the fold. Clients were waiting. There was no time for sentiment.

———

The Green Room at The Savoy was accustomed to visits from Professor Harry Lacey, as he knew Arthur Sullivan, the composer, very well. They had first met at the Beefsteak Club, where their mutual friend, the lawyer turned pianist, Corney Grain, had treated them to his favourite delicacies. On this night, the audience were eagerly anticipating a production of *The Gondoliers*, and Arthur had found time to walk with Lacey to the backstage areas, chatting all the while. Like Lacey, he relished a good meal and invited the professor to a feast the coming weekend.

'How can I turn you down, Arthur? Though I'm supposed to be losing a few pounds. I promised my doctor, and, bless him, he's always giving me lectures about surfeits of this and that. The man has no

humanity … Now, I'm looking for Miss Cabrelli …
I believe she's playing Casilda?'

Arthur stroked his moustache and gave a sigh. 'Ah,
I'm sorry to disappoint you, but Miss Cabrelli wasn't
chosen for that part. No, she had something of a *con-
tretemps* with WSG. I'm afraid she's helping with the
costume and props.'

'You mean she's been virtually dismissed?' Lacey
was indignant.

'No, no, simply in the shadows for a while, until
WSG changes his mind. She argued with him over a
song. Rather a prodigious error of judgement, Harry.
Anyway, you'll find her in here.' He opened a door
and waved his hand for Harry to enter. 'I must get to
the orchestra now. *À bientôt mon ami.*'

It was drawing close to curtain-up and most of
the performers were on their feet, pacing around the
place. The air in the room was blue with expletives
and the skivvy sitting at the back, hurriedly stitching
a few inches of seam on a very full skirt, jumped
up, startled into a response by Harry's approach as
he spoke her name. 'Dear Miss Cabrelli … lovely to
meet you again!' He looked far from bohemian, with
his bushy moustache, tousled fair hair and sober black
wool top-coat and narrow trousers. 'You were wonderful at Miss Bellezza's party last week! Now here
you are working with my friend Arthur! Well done
indeed.'

Cara, short and raven-haired, was not dressed for
the stage. Trying to look every inch the administrator,

she wore a blouse and skirt; the blouse, with puffed-up cuffs, encompassed her neck in a high collar and was making her very hot. She stood up and gave Harry a hug as the call came for the stars to move out into the limelight.

'Oh Mr Lacey, lovely to see you, but as you see, I'm in a spot of bother. I offended Mr Gilbert, but Sullivan thinks he's only sulking, as men do, and I'll be back in his good books by next week. But for now I'm backstage ... and I hate it.'

'Well, my dear, it may be that I can offer you a part in a little play for us ... for the Septimus Society ... when I hinted at some work.'

Cara jumped up, uttering a girlish giggle, and clapped her hands. 'Oh Harry! How exciting! Tell me more, do!' Harry straightened his tie, unruffling himself. He was a stranger to the attentions of women and was positively flushed.

'My dear, there is a whiff of danger about it. It's not exactly a Savoy part. But I've seen you act, and I've had excellent reports about you from others ... and basically, well, can you meet me at Holborn House auctions at eleven tomorrow? I've drawn a map here, and I've written an account of who you are – dearest Cara, you are to be an American millionaire's daughter, so dress for the part. Arthur has told me that you may borrow anything from the wardrobe here.'

'*Anything*! Oh, joy! Harry, you're my Fairy Godfather! May I kiss you?'

The professor blushed and stepped back, but he could not avoid Cara's lunge at him, and her kiss on his lips, in spite of his protest.

'Oh, I'm quite dizzy with all this, dear Cara. But tomorrow you are not Cara – you are Miss Dora Delancey. Enjoy it! Read my notes carefully ... oh, and the essential thing is that you are soft-hearted, but are to be guided by Detective Inspector Carney, who will be with you all day.'

Cara took a sharp intake of breath and said, 'Detective Inspector Carney ... a *real* detective?'

'Indeed. Now, farewell my dear. We shall meet again at the next Oriental dinner.' Harry walked briskly off, leaving Cara to recover from the shock.

—

'Now we're all set ... if I get someone back here, I have to have some notes from them, some rag, some bees and honey, right Thomas?'

Tosher, who knew that when his real name was used Ned Byrne meant business, and that some danger was afoot, nodded so much that his belly wobbled. Twice the size of Byrne he may have been, but the smaller man had the knack of instilling a deep fear, a chill that reached the bones and the viscera. Byrne reached up and grasped Tosher's jaw, pulling his face down lower so he could look him in the eye, close and threatening.

'Right Guv,' Tosher stammered out. 'We'll not come away empty, like.'

'Not even if I have to call on your skills with the knife and fetchin' someone a good whack, right?' Ned growled.

Tosher managed to nod, his face still in Byrne's grip.

'So Ned and Thomas do not end today with no shekels in the pocket, right?' Byrne smiled nastily. 'Shake on it?'

They shook hands, and Byrne knew from the slight quavering of his big servant that the fight for power had been won.

———

In the Holborn auction room the main chamber was packed with people. It was a specialist art sale, comprising only works by British artists of the eighteenth and early nineteenth centuries. There was a cluster of aristocratic looking men in one corner, enjoying cigars and brandy, and appearing to find the whole business highly amusing. In the main concourse, the men of business gathered, and most were anxiously consulting their descriptive catalogues, stroking their chins and looking around for familiar faces. Among this crowd a young woman was gently guided around the room by an older man, the couple indulging in small talk. It was Cara, *a la* Dora Delancey, and Detective Inspector Edward Carney looked every inch the distinguished man of culture – a part he found unfamiliar, but he had been tutored by Harry and in his long police career he had seen hundreds of expert swindlers who passed very well as professors, clerics or academic gentlemen.

Cara was dressed in distinctly more gaudy attire than was usual in these circles in the City, having selected an ornate and highly embellished outfit from the costume store at The Savoy. Her dress was, however, very much the current fashion of the nineties, with a scattering of little flowers embroidered across the skirt, and her bodice was tight and shaped. This had been carefully chosen with the prospect of much walking and movement ahead of her. She wore long white gloves and carried a parasol, which she considered to be useful if the need for defence arose.

Eddie's greatest challenge was to speak as if he were a 'posh type' and drop his Cockney accent. But he was used to that, and he somehow managed to adapt his voice and manner to the clothes he was wearing. 'Dress posh, talk posh,' he murmured to himself, as they walked into the Holborn rooms.

Cara made sure that her American accent was heard, and her references to some of the art around them made her seem, superficially at least, most informed regarding modern art.

A hush descended as the auctioneer appeared on a dais, gavel in hand. He began to announce the pictures and the bidding went fast and furiously, as lot followed lot. Then he came to a pause and announced, 'Now, we have a very remarkable landscape by Frederick William Canlon, one of his views of the River Thames, rather than his beloved home county where he lived, close to our dear former laureate, Lord Tennyson ...'

As everyone fixed their gaze on the auctioneer, Cara heard the soft voice of a man whisper in her ear. 'Miss, I see you are here to purchase some of our best British art ... well, I have something that may be of interest to you, not here, but in my rooms ... I'm talking about a Canlon watercolour. It's better than this one in fact, and much cheaper.'

Eddie heard this, and tugged Cara away, but the bait was taken, and he looked closely at Ned Byrne, who introduced himself as the bidding stopped. Byrne was at his most dapper, but it was his gaudy necktie that people noticed, and, of course, Eddie made a note of the glass eye and scar, wondering if the man had a record.

Over a cup of tea in the sitting room, Cara nodded encouragingly as Byrne spoke.

'Miss, the watercolour is for sale for seven hundred pounds ... but if you could pay with notes, then five hundred for you, as I have a particular admiration for our American friends.' His smile almost made Eddie sick, but he managed to look agreeable.

'Come and see it for yourselves!' Byrne said, spreading his arms wide and being the genial companion. He, too, could act.

———

Eddie and Cara were walking behind Byrne, who was setting a fast pace, and they had turned off Leadenhall Street and were heading towards

Houndsditch when at last the pace slackened. The poor light and low cloud made it difficult to see ahead, but Byrne was anxious that they moved quickly. He repeatedly apologised that his friend's studio was so far from the auction rooms, and Eddie became more and more suspicious, feeling certain now that this was their man. Finally, they arrived at a dull, rotten court off Middlesex Street and a rush of street urchins came at them. Cara wanted to give them a coin but Byrne shouted so threateningly that the children ran back into the shadows.

'No, Miss ... you have much to learn about London!' he said, directing them into a doorway.

The room itself was dark and with a low ceiling. The main source of light was from what was left of the sun – very little – and a cluster of church candles on a table top. A man wearing a dirty smock was squatting over a still life picture of fruit. Around the plaster walls, dull ochre in hue, with paint peeling off everywhere, there were frames and lumber stacked, with a few small watercolours spaced between. Clearly, Eddie thought, the crook thought that the image of a poor painter, starving in a squalid back room of a lodging house, would increase the chances of a sale, a purchase through pity, as it were.

As Byrne led Cara and Eddie in, the painter, Tosher, turned and said grumpily, 'Not another interruption, Mr Byrne. I'm putting all my best efforts into this patch of light on the apple, see ... Lord, what would my good father say to see me struggling? He had such a facility with the brush, though of course he used his finger-end very much. He always said his thumbnail was his best tool!'

'Miss Delancey, may I introduce Fred Canlon, only son of the great man.'

Cara gave a whoop of joy and Eddie, maintaining his role of cheery Cockney, said, 'By gawd, you're his flesh and blood ... son of the man himself?'

'You mean I'm standing a few feet away from the son of F.W. Canlon?' Cara gushed.

'Yes you are, Miss,' said Byrne, 'and if you turn around you will see the Canlon picture I spoke of. There it is, *View of Lincoln Cathedral from the Witham* – painted, I believe, in 1859 when Frederick was in his last year on this earth.'

The painter wiped his hands on his smock. 'Indeed, I can recall well his last months – a swan-song, of course.'

Cara was smoothly into her part of rich heiress now, and cooed over the picture like a turtle dove. 'Mr Byrne, you spoke eloquently about this at the sales, but I have to say that the real thing is beyond description ... it simply *is*, don't you agree Edward?'

Byrne and the painter were now standing with a confident air, feeling certain that they had a buyer. But Cara and Eddie knew their task, and Eddie made the first critical comment. 'Of course, Miss Delancey, we'll have to be sure. I mean, five hundred pounds is a deal of money. Your Pa would want to be sure of the investment, like, see what I mean?'

A frown appeared on Cara's sweet face and she spoke coyly: 'Oh well, Mr Byrne *is* an experienced dealer and he speaks very knowledgeably on art.'

Byrne knew when his gift of the gab was called for: 'Oh yes, I been in the trade for ... twelve years you know.'

Eddie took a few steps and looked over the other paintings. 'These by our man as well Mr Bryne?'

'All but one ... the religious subject. As I said earlier, I have landscapes by a number of British artists. I specialise in work from earlier this century, mainly to the time of our dear Queen's accession.'

'You see, Edward, he is a particular student of his area of expertise,' Cara said, patting Byrne's arm and laughing.

Eddie was ready to set the trap. 'Still, I'm here to advise you Miss Delancey, and I have to say that we first need to check on some things and return another day ... unless, Mr Byrne, we make a decision tonight and you call on us tomorrow?' They had to get Byrne to come to meet them the next day, and the best location would be the one the Society had as virtually their own – the Oriental Hotel.

Tosher, half in shadow, moved closer to Byrne and there was whispering. Then it was the turn of the artist's son to speak, and it was clear from his tone that he was not pleased. He took down the painting from the wall and ran a finger along the gold frame. 'Miss Delancey, this little picture is unique. There are people across several continents who long to possess it.

You need to think of it as not merely a monetary investment, but as a dying man's prayer to Nature. Oh yes, my dear Pa's last breaths were not far off when he laboured over this. In truth, Miss, it would not be too extreme to say that this great work of art was the cause of his death.'

Cara almost giggled, so grossly sentimental were these words, but her handkerchief came to her rescue; pulled out and placed over her mouth, it enabled her to simulate a few sobs. She dabbed her eyes and appeared to work very hard to fight back her tears. She gave a small gasp and turned away.

'How can you, Miss Delancey, as a serious collector, allow this to pass you by?' Byrne added, hanging the picture back on its hook. The painter was still in the emotional throes of his almost poetic discourse, to which Cara responded, crying, 'Bid him take it down again, do!'

'Sorry to disappoint, but this cannot be rushed,' Eddie said. 'But if you would care to come to the Oriental Hotel tomorrow, at say eleven, a decision will have been made. Our art man will need to look at some catalogues and such. I shall then pay you, other things being equal, in ready money – something we rarely do in my circles, though I did bring some with me tonight, hoping that my friend here would permit a deal.'

There was a silence which seemed to last for ages, and in that time the painter and Byrne looked at each other searchingly. Eddie was expecting a response – perhaps a new deal and a reduced price, proving their desperation. In his experience, these types would take actual bank notes even if the profit was much less than they wanted. Would they take the bait? Cara wanted to say more, but exploited the silence well, taking a few steps towards the stairs. Then, at last, Byrne said, 'Very well. Eleven tomorrow it is.'

'Then goodbye ... and Mr Canlon,' Cara paused, 'do be sure that I shall say a memorial prayer for your father. On what day did he die?' This was a masterstroke from the actress, as she and Eddie saw the painter momentarily nonplussed and confused. Then Byrne cut in, before the embarrassment grew into an unwanted aura of suspicion. 'It was December tenth of course, wasn't it Fred.'

'Yes, yes, December tenth,' stuttered the painter. 'His going was ... merciful.'

When Eddie and Cara were back on the street, they waited until they turned a corner before they both exclaimed 'Yes!' in triumph.

'I always did like fishin', Miss Cara ... and this time we maybe caught a whopper!'

Detective Inspector Edward Carney took her gloved hand and kissed it.

——

Eddie looked up and down the street. It was dark and there was practically no light to be had. Luckily he knew this part of the city fairly well. They were somewhere near Lime Street, so he reckoned that they had some walking to do. For a second, he looked around and frowned. Cara sensed his doubt.

'Eddie, are you alright? Are we lost?'

'No, not at all. You're talking to a police officer. I used to do my beat round here ... only problem is, it's very dark and it's been a long time since I did anything but paper sorting and filing. Why do you think I like to use some time with George and Harry? They do some real detective work, and my Super don't mind ... we call it a special attachment.'

They walked on and Eddie said, 'We just need to reach the Old Lady and then it's down Queen Victoria Street all the way to Blackfriars. They'll be waiting for a report at the Oriental. I don't know about you, Cara, but I need a drink!' He knew that Byrne and the 'artist' now believed that he carried some hundreds of pounds on his person, after talking about being able to pay in cash. They thought he was rich, and that was temptation enough.

He took her hand and led the way. A hundred yards further on they reached the way into a court, rather than the junction with Leadenhall Street. There was merely the slightest hint of nervousness in his voice as he said, 'Oh, wrong way my dear. Turn back ... left at the end. Sorry. They'll have me back in uniform if I carry on like this!'

Cara tried not to show any concern, but there was a noticeable thickening of the fog that muffled the street around them. There was not a sound, nothing, then one footfall, and it came from behind them. Eddie halted sharply and listened intently, trying to see who was there. 'I can only see about twenty feet. Better trust to instinct, and I'll tap the wall. We'll come to a street name and then that will be fine.'

Slowly, haltingly, they continued in what Eddie sensed was more or less a south-westerly direction , hoping that Leadenhall Street would soon appear. But in the fog that was wrapping it's chill fingers around every brick, every cobblestone, every chimney, there was another, and he was not far behind them. Out of the gloom there came a sudden scraping sound, as if a cane had rubbed against a wall.

'Who's there?' Eddie called.

Pushing Cara behind him he turned to face the invisible menace. At first there was a rustling noise, and then something seemed to fall, something light such as a hat. Suddenly a shape rushed from the dark and before he could raise his hands to guard himself, Eddie was thrown to the floor and a very heavy, solid ruffian was on him, about to strike.

'Inspector, look out!' Cara cried as she saw the club raised but in that second the man got to his feet and ran off, shouting, 'Not a bobby! I ain't gonna see off no bobby!' Cara realised that he was talking to some-one else, and she thought she heard the sound of feet running a little further away, but her first instinct was to help Eddie.

Someone shouted and a man approached. 'What street are we on?' Eddie asked him, getting to his feet.

'You're in Bury Street Sir … Cornhill's just further on this way.'

'Call a cab, man! I'm the police!'

Twenty minutes later they walked into the Oriental Hotel, where the other five members of the Septimus Society were enjoying drinks and listening to Lord George regale them with how he had narrowly escaped death at the hands of a mob in Egypt. He was leaning back from the table and the others were listening intently, drinks in hand and the meal completed. Harry Lacey had drunk too much brandy; Maria de Bellezza was urging George to describe the riot in Egypt, and Smythe was chuckling at the sheer wildness of it all. But all talk stopped when Cara and Eddie walked into the room, the detective looking notably dishevelled.

Maria went to him immediately, but he merely explained that he was fine and had simply had a 'bit of a rough do' with a footpad, but that the rogue in question was almost certainly one of the men in the artist's studio. Cara recounted the events of the evening with Byrne, as everyone retired to armchairs and whiskies were given to Cara and Eddie.

Harry felt that it was time to explain what might be done next. He leaned forward and looked around the group, inviting everyone to listen. 'Now, Septimus people, there is no possibility that the fish will now bite. The attacker tonight was obviously either Byrne or someone with him. The most likely situation is that even now, as we speak, this "studio" will have gone.

He and his accomplice will almost certainly move on elsewhere.'

'Yes. They probably move from room to room, renting a dingy little place for each fraud, keeping one step ahead of everyone!' Lord George agreed, puffing a cloud of smoke into the air.

Smythe joined in. 'Well, we must work out how to find the next studio and be waiting for the scoundrels!'

Maria de Bellezza, perhaps the most accomplished speaker and lecturer of them all, stood and addressed the group as if it were an official meeting. 'Gentlemen … and lady … I think we may assume that these men are setting up a so-called studio for each attempted sale of their fraudulent goods. Our task, therefore, is to be one step ahead and find their next most likely place for the next studio. *Si, e vero?*' She resumed her seat and George took over, though without moving from his usual languid posture.

'True, yes, I agree completely my dear Maria. My suggestion is that the next studio is likely to be either in Whitechapel or in Cheapside. They won't be anywhere close to today's location.'

'Sorry to dampen your theory, My Lord … but they'll be terrified,' interposed Jemmy Smythe. 'Even if we narrow it down to the cheapest rooms in those two areas, it's a longshot.'

'I was rather hoping we could reduce the options by noting the very cheapest lettings in the paper columns, and then deploying men to watch for arrivals,' said George.

Harry had been following the reasoning very closely. He walked across to help himself to another drink and then turned, stroked his moustache and let out a world-weary sigh. 'Ah, fellow sleuths ... I suggest that, instead of doing all this longshot work, we entice them. I have written a short piece this evening, as you were all expressing your very worthy ideas, and I can have this in the hands of my friend Wilbert at *The Times* by the morning. This is the simple paragraph.' He lifted up his notebook and read aloud:

CANLON STUDIO TO LET

We have it on good authority that Mr Earnest Delmont, the Chairman of the Dilettante Club, has acquired the very studio in which the great Watercolourist F.W. Canlon worked whilst in the City. Though celebrated for his views of Lincolnshire, Canlon also painted the Thames, notably at Wapping, and the studio is very close to Wapping Basin, at the corner of Well Street. Persons wishing to rent should contact Mr Delmont at the Dilettante, Haymarket.

Cries of 'Well done Harry!' cheered the literary bachelor far more than any applause he had received after seminars on Kit Marlowe or even the Bard himself.

'Just one small point – won't the bounders be a touch suspicious, reading this so soon after tonight's little business?' It was Eddie, ever the rational Peeler.

'Fair point ... but we shall have to hope that the men's greed overcomes their caution, because if they had that studio, with this press cutting in their hand, think of the appeal to buyers!' Harry beamed at his plan. 'There will be, of course, no such place, but we shall be at that address with Mr Delmont, after enquiries.'

'We'll be there as soon as the piece is in the paper,' said Eddie. 'Believe me, our swindlers will be there right away, to survey the place.'

———

It was around midday when Byrne and Tosher arrived at Well Street, and they were not alone. There was a small crowd there, some of the number gathered having notebooks, and there was also a photographer setting up. All eyes were on the first-floor window, and everyone listened to Harry, who was, for the day only, Mr Delmont of the Dilettante Club. He wore his most gaudy waistcoat, and a tie verging on the loud and assertive. Even his usual grey coat had been abandoned and replaced by a light fawn sports jacket, and on his head was a checked cloth bowler hat. His Cambridge friends would not have recognised him.

'Gentlemen, you are gazing at the very room. Observe the long window for the necessary light, and that neat little balcony ... an Italianate touch for our great artist. As you know, he painted the English rising of autumn sunrise amazingly well ...'

'We must get the place, Tosher,' Byrne said. 'Think of the pull of that address! The rent would be a sound investment. We'd appear honest and legitimate in the actual, approved studio!' Byrne insisted on boldly walking across to join the crowd, but Tosher, nervous, dropped back.

The crowd had moved in close to Harry, who was standing on a box so he could be seen as he spoke. In the middle of his speech, he saw Byrne approach – he matched Cara's description very well, even down to the green cravat. Harry gave the nod and before Byrne could move, he was held by two pairs of strong arms and he turned to see two police constables, fixing their glare on him.

'Mr Byrne, I believe?' said Harry, and immediately Byrne shouted, 'Tosher … help!' but the big man was already running. From behind Harry, Eddie ran out, followed by two more officers, all giving chase to Tosher.

'This will be the man who attacked me, boys!' yelled Eddie.

Tosher, in sheer panic, took a right turn into Smithfield. He was heavily built but he could gather some speed, and was soon on the edge of St Katherine's Dock. Moving quickly he lunged for the first turning that appeared, and found himself running through an arched siding, like a dank tunnel, with massive beer barrels on both sides of him. A shout from behind called, 'You – stop there! This is the law!'

He ran but felt his pace slowing. 'No, not inside again … I will not go back into that black hell! I will not!'

His heart was thumping so hard he felt the echo in his throat. He turned to see his pursuers, but in that second he took a sidestep and hit a rack holding a barrel. The massive bulk of it rolled into the side of his leg and he was knocked six feet aside, as the weight settled on an ankle. Tosher heard the running footsteps coming nearer and nearer. Only twenty feet ahead was the edge of the dock and the pool of water beyond. With one last effort of strength he pulled free of the barrel's rim and crawled to the water's edge.

Eddie Carney was ahead of his men, wanting to grab the man who had meant to kill him just two nights ago. He saw the huge figure teetering on a fence and then the man's weight fell forward and lurched towards the brown water. Tosher had time to turn, so that Eddie saw his face, and the detective heard the big man cry, 'I'm not going back, bobby, I'm not going back in there!'

A Thief in the Night

'Really, Lacey, you have none of the skills required for billiards!' said the tall aristocrat as the white ball slammed against the cushion and bounced into the air. He and his friend, Professor Harry Lacey of Cambridge, were enjoying a game at the Septimus Club. Lacey merely smiled, enjoying the ribbing. His long hair flopped into his eyes and his pince-nez slipped rather when he tried to concentrate on a shot.

'Well I've had enough for tonight, George ... too tired,' he said, absentmindedly chalking the tip of his cue. 'Been trying to construe seventeenth-century manuscripts all day, until you called and rescued me. The men of those benighted times loved their fusty, musty paper and tended to spill eggs and cheese all over their poems. That, on top of being too enthusi-astic in dealing with a very large luncheon with some dons up in town. Anyway, look at you, six feet and more of youth and suavity, played billiards since you were a young blade, and me a middle-aged bookman with short sight! Perhaps you would like a game of chess – far more up my street old man!'

His associate was Lord George Lenham-Cawde, and he could never resist teasing his friend. After all, he was well aware that, as they stood in the billiard room of the Septimus Club in Piccadilly, his friend was a rather shabby, tweed-clad bachelor still living like a vicar in his Cambridge rooms, while he himself had the funds to buy half of the university if he wished. 'Lacey old man, why on earth do you waste time on old paper? That's all you do ... mess about with smelly old yellow paper!'

'Oh stop it, George, you know you're jealous. You are as bored as an old dowager in her knitting circle, and you have to have a go at me to raise a smile. I love my work. Fine, so you wear a Savile Row suit and shoes that shine like a horseman's breeches, but are you happy? I'm jolly happy with old poems. You know where you are with them ... unlike people, with whom you have something of an unhealthy preoccupation, I might add. I prefer my work.'

'Ah yes, your work ... I tried to read your dull tome on the sonnets of Shakespeare. I dropped off to sleep at page two. Sorry and all that ...'

At that moment the door was burst open and a stout, red-faced man of around sixty came in, with Smythe behind him, calling out apologies.

'I'm terribly sorry Lord Lenham-Cawde, but he pushed past me and ...'

'Not to worry Smythe ... leave us to have a chat with our desperate friend.'

As Smythe left, the visitor advanced angrily towards Lenham and grabbed his collar. 'By heaven Sir, you have defiled my daughter and you will pay … every court in the land … every court I tell you. I have powerful friends.'

Lord George, who was a foot taller than the assailant, pulled himself free of his grasp and smiled. 'I have no idea who you are … but this is my friend, Professor Harry Lacey. Let's sit shall we?'

The man responded with a shout and then loosened his collar. 'You are beneath contempt Sir … my heart is racing … and I am not a well man, I may add.'

At that point, Lacey intervened and led the man to a sofa, spoke gently to him and offered him a gin from the tray of drinks on the side-table. Lord George sat opposite, lit a cheroot and crossed his long legs.

'Now, who are you, and who is your daughter?'

'I am Charles Perch of Richmond … you know very well who I am. You are Lord Albert Lenisham?'

Before Lord George could reply, Professor Lacey spoke up. 'No you buffoon, this is Lord George Lenham-Cawde! You are mistaken and have made a grave error, Sir. I suggest you apologise.'

Perch put down his drink. There was a flush across his face and he stood, then walked across to George and bent forward, almost as if to curtsey. 'My deepest apologies, My Lord … I was misinformed. I'm so awfully sorry…'

Lord George stood and patted him on the shoulder. 'Hey … no harm done old chap. We all get things wrong at times. Sounds as if you've a little problem there. Some cad seduced your daughter?'

'It's a long story … but I think we have a villain abroad. This Lord Albert Lenisham must be found! He is a philanderer of the first order. I've never met the man, but I've heard all about him from my daughter. He's been working his charms on her this last two months or so … been to Ascot, been to the theatre … taken her to Boulogne once. But the devil never shows his face in Richmond. I got the names mixed up … don't know what I'm doing half the time!'

'What else can you tell us about this man? Lacey asked.

'All I know is that Alice says she loves him … and then, this week, well, she shows all the signs of being … well, *with child*!

Lord George took a sip of his whisky and then, waving Perch to sit down again, he spoke with care, in his most judicious manner. 'I'm afraid that there is no Lord Lenisham. Lord Albert died two years ago, and he had no family … no sons, no heir. Very sad. It seems that you have been the victim of a fraud. This bounder who charmed your daughter, he's most likely a seasoned rogue. If you could give us a description we may be able to help. Eh Lacey?'

'Well, let me see,' Perch blustered, 'I gather he's short, rather rotund … smokes cigars and … he has wavy blonde hair and, oh my God!' A look of horror filled his face. He had suddenly had some kind of epiphany, and it wasn't a good one.

'Oh my dear Lord Lenham-Cawde … the crook may be at my home now! The place is empty now … as we speak. My daughter Alice is with her aunt in Oxford, as she is ill!'

Lacey asked, 'Surely he can't get in?'

'Would he have a reason to get in?' Lord George asked. 'I mean … are you a particularly wealthy man Mr Perch? One hates to mention money, but in this case it seems to apply.'

'Well, yes … I mean, I'm retired from my hotel business. I own a hotel by the sea … the Calsworth … and well, I live a quiet life really.'

Lacey stepped in with a direct question, 'Do you keep money at home?'

Perch was visibly sweating now and he took out a handkerchief and dabbed his forehead with it, mumbling a mix of laments and curses. Then he said, 'Well, no, very little … but I do have … oh no! My collection of guns. He wouldn't! I have a very valuable collection of pistols…. I have a room full of Parkers … of Holborn, you know? I have around forty of them … and some rare duelling pistols too. Been collecting them since I was twenty, forty-odd years ago now. He wouldn't be after those surely?'

Lord George spoke, even as he picked up his coat from the stand, 'Parkers? I know the ones. He may be more than a cad … he may be out for something else. What about your servants? Are they at home?'

'No … I have none living in, and I am a widower. Two local ladies do all the cleaning. I don't live a grand life, as I say. No butlers or anything grand!'

'There's no time to be lost,' declared Lord George. 'Let's get to Richmond … Lacey, have Smythe call a cab, now!'

———

Seconds after arriving at Shering House, Richmond, all three men were standing in a small ante-room of Mr Perch's home, beside the spacious library, surrounded by cabinets, displays and wall-mounted cases containing weapons of all kinds. Nothing appeared to have been touched or disturbed.

'Well, there are no signs of a forced entry, Mr Perch. It appears that all is well,' Professor Lacey said, tapping the glass top of a long display case. 'Your home is indeed, it appears, your castle!'

'Yes, thanks to providence eh?' Charles Perch sighed and offered his guests a drink. 'Please take a seat … here, gentlemen, please.' He motioned to a comfortable sofa and then fetched drinks from the corner. Lacey glanced along the shelves, noting the rare sets of eighteenth-century works, and a few of what appeared to be beautiful solid folios of topography in a special collection.

'You have a marvellous collection, Mr Perch,' he said, accepting the proffered whisky.

'Yes. I'm very fond of Dr Johnson and his circle. I collect them quite, what should I say … avidly.'

Lord George stretched out his long legs and looked around the room. Unlike Lacey, he had no interest in the books and furniture. What he saw was the small detail, and there was one of these which he disliked. 'Oh dear ... Mr Perch, I fear you have not noticed that little heap of papers over there.' He pointed to a corner which could not be seen from where Perch sat. The man immediately dashed over to investigate, and the others followed.

'Well ... I can't tell what might have gone or what should be there. Though it is my financial cabinet that appears to have been raided.'

'Any money taken? Bills?'

'I wouldn't know. Alice sees to all that. She's my accounts clerk you see, bless her. She's very organised. Everything in its place.'

They all stood, staring at the pile of papers. Lord George's mind was working hard. 'Clearly, Mr Perch, this cabinet has been searched. Someone knew what they were looking for, as nothing else has been touched as far as we may tell. No door has been forced. Nothing, it seems, is amiss here.'

'I'll check upstairs, Mr Perch, if you wish?' Lacey suggested, and the man nodded. The professor walked from room to room, taking in the grand, broad landing, wide enough for children to play. But this was no house for the young. In fact it was peculiarly undisturbed. There were shining dressers, shelves and cupboards everywhere, and the solid walls were positively crammed with paintings, mostly watercolours of English rural and seafront scenes. He noticed one very large drawing of the Calsworth

Hotel, Brighton. This was obviously the place owned by Mr Perch. Lacey noticed the name of the artist at the bottom left – no less a person than Humphrey Coppice RA. Everything in the house suggested the best, as if everything Perch placed in his home was permanent – something for the future. 'Nothing ever gets moved,' Lacey murmured to himself. 'It's like ghosts live here.' Then, catching himself, he started back down the staircase when he felt a chilly draught at his neck. Turning, he spied an open window.

Lacey took a closer look. It had been forced with something hard and sharp. There was a dent and a rough edge where some wood had been forced from the frame. There was a telltale boot-print on the stair. It was a clumsy job. He called for the others.

'Yes, a rough fellow, desperate ... not a professional burglar Mr Perch,' Lord George said.

Perch was now curious. 'Lord George ... what exactly is it that you do?'

'I'm rich as Croesus. I don't do anything except play. My father left me four properties and a large slice of Wiltshire. But I do, however, have a hobby. I study criminals, as does Professor Lacey here, and I have to tell you that this does not make sense...'

He was interrupted by the slam of the front door and then a woman's voice calling up the stairs, 'What doesn't make sense? Who are these men, Papa?'

It did not take long for Alice to confess that she had been waiting for the man she knew as Lord Lenisham at Paddington, where he was supposed to meet her from the Oxford train. As she told her father the sad story, she felt sure she had been deserted by the man, as Lord Lenisham, at Paddington, where he was supposed to meet her. Lord George was watching her, beginning to understand why she would attract men. Alice was petite, fair-haired, with the complexion of an English rose – healthy, with an adorable face. Somehow, even swaddled in a heavy coat, he almost fell for her himself, but then that was something he did rather easily, and he had to pull himself up and ask a question.

'Dear Miss Perch, this man … could you describe him for me?'

'Are you a police officer? Who are these men Papa?' she asked again.

Lacey explained before anyone else could speak. 'Miss Perch, I am Professor Harry Lacey, and this is my friend, Lord Lenham-Cawde.'

She frowned. 'What? Not another lord! Believe me I've had enough of aristocrats! William … he was … he …' Here she began to sob, and her father put his arm around her shoulder and gently guided her into the nearest sitting room, followed by Lord George and Lacey.

After a strong drink, Alice gradually began to put her words together, as the men listened. 'He was lovely – very kind to me. I thought that I had found my future husband … we became very close. He was so charming, my William. But this last week he changed …'

'Alice, was this because … I mean … are you, that is to say … are you *enceinte* my dear?'

She looked up at her father sharply, 'Papa, I am *not* pregnant!'

'I am sorry to be the serious paterfamilias, but I dread to think …' Perch was about to give a lecture on morality but Alice interrupted him. 'Papa, you tried to prevent my career on the stage … all that talk about it being for fallen women! Really … I am a legitimate actress and have appeared in some classical roles … you could have encouraged me!'

Perch proceeded to give his guests a talk on the lamentable fate of most young ladies who tried to make a living by treading the boards, but Lord George cut in and moved the focus back to the break-in.

He asked them to follow him to the pile of papers spilled on the floor. 'Alice, I understand that you are in charge of the financial papers … could you have a look at this and tell me what you think is missing please.'

She crouched down and busied herself going through the bundles, which were all labelled and tied with string. Perch was still in a nervous state, and he sat back, his bulk in a rocking chair, but his heart was less agitated now that he knew there was to be no embarrassment landed on his good name.

'Ah here … there is one paper missing, Lord Lenham-Cawde … a contract, relating to the services maintaining the hotel at Brighton, our hotel … the Calsworth.'

'Miss Perch, what did your Lord Lenisham look like, may I ask?'

'Oh he's about thirty, fair hair ... oh, he smoked those foreign cigarettes with the black paper ... I thought his accent was northern ... anyway, why bother describing him? I have a drawing.'

Lacey gave a positive yelp of amazement. 'My dear young lady, you can draw as well as act?'

'My daughter is creative in every way, Professor ... including in her use of truth and lies!'

Ignoring the remark, Alice went into the library and returned with a sketchpad. George and Lacey studied the portrait and gasped at the same time.

'It's J.C. ... to the life! Jimmy Canter!'

Lord George grabbed Lacey by the arm. 'There is no time to be lost ... Harry, to your library immediately. We're looking for a scoundrel of the first order. It may be J.C. himself and his damned brother!'

They left Perch and Alice calling after them, Lord George apologising for the swift departure even as he strode out. Alice's cab was still there, and the driver shouted out, asking when he was likely to be paid.

'You will be remunerated when you have my friend at Edwardes Square, Kensington, and me at the Septimus Club, and we want to be there in no more than ten minutes!'

With a curse of 'Ruddy la-di-da ...' the driver cracked his whip and they were off.

In the dark interior of the cab, Lord George briefed his friend. 'Harry, you're looking for frauds and conmen and, in particular, our old friends the Canters, yes?'

'Yes, George … whoever he was, he wanted Perch's signature.'

'Indeed. Come to the Septimus as soon as you have found anything. I'll be planning tomorrow's watch. We shall be at the Bank of England, western office.'

———

Harry Lacey's London rooms in Edwardes Square were in complete contrast to his Cambridge study. The scholarly bachelor relished his London life, and his den in Kensington was his retreat, his bolt-hole when he needed to be out of the Cambridge stuffiness he needed but also only tolerated for so long and no more.

He had a room for dining, a small back bedroom, a basement where his ageing housemaid did the cleaning and cooking, and then there was his library. It contained only works on the history of crime. Legal reports, press cuttings and pictures, all related to the London underworld and to the corresponding, often corrupt, milieu of the wealthy. Many men in the new, brash city, a metropolis which was the hub of a massive world empire, were so hungry for money and power that they threw all morality out of the window. Lacey, a specialist in Elizabethan poetry, had developed a passion for the grisly tales in the annals of crime after meeting Lord George Lenham-Cawde at a bachelor party given to celebrate his lordship's return from India, where he had been involved in espionage against the Russians. The two men discovered a mutual penchant for hanging narratives and detective tales.

'Now then ...' he mumbled to himself as he flicked through the files on forgers and frauds relating to the last five years in London. He found 'Canter: James and Jack.' There was his meticulous summary, drawn from newspaper reports, personal enquiries and from the best source of all, the street-corner men who saw everything and heard everything, then wanted money for the information.

He was reading the notes when there was a shout from downstairs.

'Hello? Mr Lacey Sir, are you wantin' any choclit?' It was Mrs Sledge, the housemaid. He knew she would come to the door, as she always did, unable to resist being nosey if he had been out anywhere, and indeed there was a knock at the door and Mrs Sledge walked in, tutting about the bad light. 'You'll ruin your eyes Professor. Now I s'pose you bin out lecturin' and that? You and your bloomin'poetry. Funny way to make a livin' I say. Or have you bin playing the jack?'

Lacey was trying to concentrate. 'Mrs Sledge, I'm not in a talkative mood ... and I might be playing the jack, but I haven't time to tell you about it.' He made a mental note of her use of slang, reminding himself to investigate the origins of the word *jack* later when matters were resolved.

'Ooh, detective work eh? On the trail of a killer?'

'Mrs Sledge, would you be a dear and make me some strong tea? I need to keep awake and I need some peace, thank you.'

She was small, a sparrow of a woman, wearing a flowery apron, her long black hair held tight in a bun. This wobbled a little when she was in a mood, as she was now. 'Right, well I knows where I stands then. I'll put the kettle on … oh, and I expect you'll not be interested in the gent as was 'ere earlier, asking for you?'

'What? Who was it?'

'That p'liceman, the one what is always happy. Not natural that, being always happy.'

Lacey knew she meant Eddie Carney, and that was good news. The Detective Inspector had obviously been informed of the situation by someone. He had come around at exactly the right time.

'Good, now is there any possibility that there might be some tea available before Christmas?'

'Blinkin' impertinence …' Lacey heard her grumble as she left the room and headed downstairs. She loved their banter.

———

Late that night, Lord George was back in Richmond. He was led into the drawing room and given whisky. When he drank the glass straight down and refused to sit, Perch was worried.

'What on earth is it My Lord?'

'Mr Perch, I need the services of your daughter, urgently!'

Perch's double chin quivered and he blinked in such a way that Lord George started to blink also.

'Look, I said she was an actress but …'

'No you damned fool … I need her to help find this impostor.' He immediately apologised for his language, aware that he could be petulant when in a hurry.

Alice was called in from the library, where she was trying to forget her lover by reading the most sensational periodical she could find.

She had changed her clothes and was wearing a beautiful long black dress and some very colourful slippers. George was, for a moment, mesmerised by her angelic looks – the ice-grey eyes and the fair hair, and that flush on her cheeks. He thought again, *Ah, the sweetest English rose, lovelier even than before.* He could see that Jimmy Canter had chosen the Perches so that he could enjoy her favours, and as a bonus to his real reason for inveigling himself into the family.

'Yes, Lord Lenham-Cawde?'

'Please, call me George. Now, Alice, I have a part for you, in a little drama I have written myself. Are you game?'

Perch started to puff out his cheeks and grunt but Alice cut in. 'Papa … please, leave me be this time!'

He left, huffing and puffing, saying that he washed his hands of the business.

'Alice, do you wish to help trap your rogue? For I'm pretty sure I know his real identity.'

'Well, yes … how does the acting come into it?'

'My dear Miss Perch, our play is to take place at the western branch of the Bank of England at nine o'clock tomorrow, and you are to be there at that time, in disguise.'

'Disguise? Oh how exciting! Are we out to get our man?'

'Indeed ... and he will be, unless I am much mistaken, your ex-lover, the blackguard known to the police as James Canter, a fraudster. I have a feeling he is trying for the grandest prize of his dark career this time.'

'What should I do?'

'Alice, my dear,' he took her hand and squeezed it gently, 'you are, I believe, going to see this man in the bank tomorrow. It is imperative that you simply watch him and listen very closely to everything he says. In fact, if you are bold enough ... you may befriend him ... your disguise must be impenetrable so that he does not recognise you.'

She moved away and took some steps towards the window, where she mused for a moment. Then she thought of something and smiled. 'My dear Lord Len ... George ... I have the very thing. I have a costume in which a woman may be buried, complete with fox collar and a net across the face. I shall also colour my face ... as when I played Gypsy Lara in *The Spanish Goblet*. How does that sound?'

'It sounds splendid – if you're sure you can keep command of your feelings, if you see my point?'

'Oh yes, George, oh yes. Revenge is sweet, don't they say?' She forced a broad smile and held out her hand.

Lord George shook her hand, as if they were two gentlemen settling a business deal.

———

In a dark corner of the Old Coach in Covent Garden that night, Professor Lacey bought Eddie Carney a drink and listened to what the Detective Inspector had to say. Eddie stood only a few inches over five feet and his face was hidden under such a mop of thick black hair that few could make it out and give any account of him. He also wore dark clothes, regardless of where he was. Lacey thought of him as the 'Shadow' and sometimes called him that. It was surely a useful skill for a plainclothes man.

'I came earlier to tell you that the American detective is in town … whatsisname … the one what came last year after that counterfeit crowd from France.'

'You mean Harness, the Pinkerton man?'

'Harness, that's it! He's a hard nut that one. Anyway, my mates down the station was sayin' how there's a big show on, something top order. So I been watching and sloping around and I got sumfin … just a sniff like.'

'What are you sniffing, Eddie? It wouldn't be a name like Canter would it?'

Eddie's mouth dropped open. 'Gawd Prof Harry … you're on the wager, mate. You had another jack working for ya?'

There it was again – *jack*. He gave his friend a querulous look. 'Eddie, take this. I owe you this from the

Thames Police affair.' He slid a roll of notes across the table. 'Now it's all happening at the western branch of the Old Lady tomorrow, just after doors opening. If you could be on the door ready to take this man, you'd be due a glass or two of the best malt at the next Oriental dinner, old friend. But his brother is almost sure to be there, so bring Bill. We'll need his fists.'

Eddie chuckled. 'Bill ... there's an irony! Bills of exchange, Prof ... they bin forgin' em ... yes, they know all about bills.'

'Exactly! That's George's notion too. So you brought the signature?'

Eddie delved into his pocket and grabbed a small sheet of paper. 'There you are ... read that!'

The name written in a messy hand, but just readable, was Charles A C Perch, followed by a squiggle.

'Perfect – though slightly questionable!' said Lacey. 'See you tomorrow.'

They didn't shake hands. Only lawyers and barristers called at the Old Coach, and so they were mostly clear there, but you still had to be careful.

———

The massive door swung open and the commissionaire smiled as he welcomed the gentleman into the Bank of England foyer. 'Good morning Mr Perch. Lovely day!'

Mr Perch dropped a silver coin into the man's hand and walked at a stately pace up to the cashier's counter, where he was met by Major Gavin, the bank manager and the teller. However, before the major could speak, a woman bumped into them, before apologising and giving copious thanks as Mr Perch bent down to help pick up her things. As they did so, Major Gavin was called away by a tall man in a corner. It was Lord George, and he was there to distract the bank manager.

As they spoke, Major Gavin kept glancing across at Perch, but the slim man in the long tweed coat was seemingly distracted by his new female acquaintance.

'Miss, I am sorry to have to rush you,' said Perch, 'but I'm here on business and I have to see Major Gavin.'

The woman was adept at her art – that of chatting and distracting, while extracting a pocketbook from his overcoat. But it was not to steal. No, it was to make an opening to speak his name. The pocketbook was dropped on the floor, and then, as she picked it up, she said loudly, 'Oh, Lord Lenham-Cawde, you almost lost this!'

Several heads turned to look. As for 'Perch', he knew in a second who the woman was, and would have darted for the door but for the fact he was cool enough to play the game for a little longer.

'This woman is a drunk ... an habitual criminal, and she tried to steal my pocketbook!'

It seemed to work. The bulky commissionaire moved towards her and took one of her arms.

Lord George stepped forward and addressed the crowd. 'Gentlemen, *I* am Lord George Lenham-Cawde, formerly of the Guards, and this man in the rather brash and tasteless coat is not Mr Perch. He is, in fact, Mr James Canter, a noted fraudster!'

As the assembled company made the appropriate sounds of astonishment, a man in the crowd in the foyer, looking rather like the fake 'Perch' but with a fuller figure, moved to the door and slid out.

'Harry … Eddie … come in please!' Lord George shouted. There was the sound of a scuffle and some cries outside before ex-boxer Bill Crooks dragged the Jack Canter back into the foyer. George told Eddie to give Major Gavin the paper. The major took it, looked closely at it, and then glared at Mr Perch as if his eyes would pop.

'This is James Canter, not your Mr Perch. He's been busy across in New York as well, forging bills of exchange. Hold him tight there men!'

Canter was firmly in the grip of Bill and Eddie now. 'I've done nothing!' he spat. 'Lord George … I should have finished you last year in Edinburgh!'

That night in the Septimus Club, the real Charles Perch was the guest of Lenham-Cawde and Harry Lacey. Lord George explained things to him.

'You see, Mr Perch, James Canter became you. He had your address and all your personal details … then all he had to have was your signature, so he could put it on a forged bill of exchange. His brother – Jack – is the penman, the forger. Jimmy is the actor.

They usually make a formidable pair. But this time they came up against some old enemies – us!'

'The Septimus Society?' Perch asked.

'Look around you at the men in these commodious armchairs, Sir,' said Harry. 'What do they have in common? They are all – either in reality or metaphorically – seventh sons of aristocrats. You know the situation: the older sons go to the army, the law, parliament, the cloth. By the time you reach the seventh, what on earth are they to do? Now, usually they play billiards, go to the races, visit ladies of the night, frequent the theatre …'

'You're not referring to my Alice again?' interrupted Perch.

'No Sir, but you see the point? Well, some of these men want something a little more challenging. Crime offers them a challenge, notably more interesting that the Derby or the latest Gilbert and Sullivan, don't you see? This is the Septimus Club, and some of us here tonight are the Septimus Society! I myself am a seventh son. Lord Lenham-Cawde is a Lord because six elder siblings perished in imperial outposts. Even Smythe is a seventh child. Our lady members, however, are only metaphorically Septimuses. We meet for dinner at a place where ladies may join us! Fittingly, there are seven of us, and our rules say that there may never be more than seven.'

Perch was puzzled, and he asked the question the investigators had heard many times before: 'What about the police?'

Lord George chuckled. 'What about them? We have one of them as a member, and that's very useful. Raise your glass to our members who cannot be here tonight: Eddie, who has police work to do, and to Leo, who is probably dreaming up another ridiculous spy story. They are in the Society too!'

'These bills of exchange ...' Perch started.

'Oh, well, you see Major Gavin had been fooled by James Canter into thinking he was you. So he introduced him as a client to the Bank of England – that means that he can have a bill cashed on demand,' Harry explained.

'My God! How much was this bill for?'

Lord George managed a wry smile. 'Three thousand pounds sterling ... he told Major Gavin that he needed to pay a number of foreign contractors in notes. He's so damned clever he almost got away with it.'

There was something worrying Harry. 'May I mention one thing, dear George? I mean, why did Canter break into Mr Perch's house? He had had lots of opportunity to steal when he was courting Alice.'

'Ah,' said Lord George, 'here we come to the interesting aspect of the case. You see for all his exotic cigarettes and expensive suits, Canter loves burgling! His father was a safe-breaker, and his uncle a robber of the night streets ... Mr Canter liked to enter premises. I first came across him while staying at Edinburgh with an old school friend, a lawyer who told me all about Canter and his gang ... they

moved South since then, hoping to be unknown here, of course. Anyway, he knew that Alice was away and that you were out too, Mr Perch. He had the thrill of getting in without passing through an opened door. I'll wager a thousand notes that he never asked Alice for a key ... not even when he was almost a son-in-law and father of your grandchild Sir!'

Perch scowled and grumbled to himself, but he raised a glass.

As they enjoyed their drinks, the Canter brothers were sitting in a police cell, cursing Lord George and his 'dirty lot of stuffy Lord Mucks!'

The Torment of Memory

Richmond Street, St John's Wood, was ideally placed for a patron of the arts to live, and on an October day in 1891 the mistress of number 5 had had her servants and cook busy since dawn. Her expected guests included a lord, a noted poet and a number of respected actors, the latter being hard to find, as most of that profession were considered to be beneath consideration for social events of a high tone. The house was ideal for the kinds of artistic events that tended to be held there, having a multitude of small corners and alcoves, sitting rooms and garden rooms; there was even an inner atrium, copying the Roman ideal of strolling and mentally relaxing among little groves of shrubs and flowers, with the city left far away and out of mind.

In the large sitting room, Maria de Bellezza's *conversazione* was going very well. The afternoon tea had been served and the drinks were being given out by her manservant. She took advantage of a lull in the conversation, while drinks were taken and sipped, to look around. The young poet was suitably voluble and self-concerned; the Dowager Fenlon was busy with stories of Paris scandals in her youth, and the classical pianist was patting the shoulder of the *bel canto* tenor. But poor Lord Lenham-Cawde looked rather melancholy. There he was, legs stretched out as usual, too long for any decent mode of relaxation, she thought. He would have to be cheered up.

Everyone was standing and the newcomers – mostly actors and writers – were nodding and smiling, playing the responsive rather than the active parts in the cut and thrust of chat. This meant that she could walk through and look down on the one solitary seated guest.

'Why George, why so down and dismal? Has there been a death in the family?' Lord George Lenham-Cawde was simply George here, in a place he loved, surrounded by talk of ideas and beliefs, revolutions and celebrations, but on this day he was down in the mouth. 'I do beg your pardon, Maria, but yes, I am troubled. Someone from the past has returned … '

Maria was a woman with a past; she had lived and she had suffered. But she chose to laugh whenever she could, and on this occasion she tried to cheer up her friend. She was one of those women who are always radiant, always the cause of smiles and good cheer wherever she found herself. She was beautiful, not pretty. She had what many thought to be classic Italian beauty: a full figure, and a face like a courtesan from a Fragonard painting. Her smile, many thought, would melt a heart of stone. Maria had known just one husband but many lovers, and had been a society hostess in several European capitals; her husband had been the Margrave of Karnesheim, and she had learned grace, manners and discretion from the best courtiers in France and in Austria.

'This person, George – is it a woman?'

'Of course.'

'But you are a man of the world … surely this is nothing too serious?'

'Maria, the truth is that I loved her, and she loved me. I have never forgotten her, but I had assumed that fate had stepped in and that she would have a husband by now … probably in St Petersburg.'

'Oh Heaven – she's Russian?' Maria winced dramatically.

'Yes. She's Irina Danova, the singer.'

'Irina Danova! Why, she's celebrated from Madrid to Moscow and from Paris to Prague. Her voice is a divine gift, George. In fact, I once met her at a soirée given by the Duchesse de Madancourt. All eyes were fixed on her the entire evening!'

Before George could speak, a voice cut through all the small talk and made heads turn. It was the young poet, an aesthete, holding a lily. He asked everyone to sit down and gave them notice that he was to read a poem. 'Now, let's talk of love, my friends, the one blessing in a world of sorrows. Why, I hold that poetry tells beautiful lies in an ugly world and ugly truths in a beautiful world, and therefore, as we live amongst the ugliness of the great horror of London, I speak of beauty.' He flicked a lock of auburn hair from one eye and began to recite. The assembled crowd were silent and attentive, and as his last line – 'And so a woman's beauty saves us all from our failures' – was spoken, George stood up and walked briskly from the room, whispering an apology to Maria.

He loitered outside for some time, unable to decide what to do next. His instinct was to find a dark hole and hide there, like a wounded animal. George knew that, as had happened to him at other times in life, notably out East in the hill country, the feeling was of a black shadow over him, the arrival of the past, which never really stays where it should be.

———

Later, at the Septimus Club, Lord George was dozing on his usual sofa, a book on his knee, when Harry walked in and woke his friend with a hearty hullo. He dropped a letter on George's knee. 'Picked it up as I came in … Smythe said it had just arrived.'

'Oh, it's what I expected!'

'Why aren't you playing billiards in there George? Young Tabby Culhorn's taking on all-comers at a fiver a go and you could beat him surely?' Harry asked, as his friend opened the letter, read it, and then put it away in an inside pocket.

'Something wrong, you great skulking aristocrat?'

George took a cigarette from its case and waited until it was lit before replying. 'Sit down, Harry, if you have a while to listen.'

'Of course. Whatever's the matter?'

When Harry was settled and attentive, George gave a deep sigh and said, 'An affair of the heart, Harry.'

'Well, that's nothing new for you old boy … only last January you were pursuing that horse-riding woman back in Lincolnshire.'

'Oh Harry, that was a *jeu d'esprit* … a trifle. This is the real thing. You have brought me a note from Irina Danova. Need I say more? Your copious memory will recall I have spoken of her before.' His friend's face was blank. 'Very well, you have forgotten. Well, I met Irina when I was in Persia back in '85. God, Harry, she took my soul away! Now here she is in London, five years later, inviting me to a recital. She's singing classical *lieder* at the Steinway Hall tomorrow evening.'

'Well George, that's a fine thing, surely? I can hum along with Arthur's tunes at The Savoy every day of the week, but *lieder* … that's another thing!'

'Really Harry, enough about the damned *lieder*! Oh, I'm sorry. Keep to your sonnets and your odes, Harry. Love is not in your vocabulary is it? Have you ever felt the pain of the kind of love that eats at you? I've tried to forget her and failed miserably. My mind is constantly of her … I feel her close to me, sense her perfume, merely talking of her to you now. Now here she is, on my doorstep, as it were.'

'You couldn't be more wrong old man. I may be the ageing bachelor today, but I was once engaged to be wed … some years ago now. I never told you.'

George suddenly sat forward, stubbed out his cigarette and gave Harry a little punch on the shoulder. 'Well, you old critic, you – you're a dark horse. What happened … she got bored of your lectures on Sir Philip Sidney?'

'She died. Pneumonia.'

George was shocked and struggled for words, such was the shame rising in him. 'I'm so sorry, Harry, I had no idea.'

'Well how could you? Enough said. Tell me about this Irina will you.'

'Even better … read this while I go and challenge our Tabby Culhorn, the brazen little beggar. Look at the pages for June 1885. No one else has ever seen this, Harry. But I know that you will understand, that you will respond with feeling and integrity.' He tossed the book onto Harry's knee. It was a leather-bound travel journal, with *Lord Lenham-Cawde: Journal 1883-6* written in longhand on the cover panel. 'I was young and foolish then, Harry, but my emotions were sure, and they never took the world lightly.'

The book had clearly been on its travels: it was stained with unspeakable colours of revolting origin; the corners were dog-eared, and there were ink-blots evident everywhere, but he found the right page and read:

June 2 1885, Tehran

Being still suffering from the knife wound to my thigh on the last Sudan assignment, I have to spend some time here, and God is smiling on me in that delay. Irina is here, having three weeks' stay with M. Couron, the French ambassador.

She has agreed to sing in a series of concerts for the Pasha, but has ample time for recreation. We have renewed our acquaintance, as I met her in Paris last year.

My heart leapt to see her. Memories of our time in Paris came flooding back, filling my imagination with scenes of sheer joy. To think that Carstairs and the other officers are all up in Afghanistan while I linger here, enjoying what some would call the dalliance of the young lover.

Irina Danova is the sweetest creature, born to delight, distract, seduce — everything a woman should do who knows and values her own exceptional charms. Many women are attractive but few have the true beauty of ideal form. She is of middle height, with auburn hair curled down to her shoulders; her eyes are brown and her form that of a young woman newly emerged from gauche girlhood to true feminine perfection.

Every man of wealth and standing here fancies that she could be either his wife or his mistress. Many adore her and flock to her concerts to worship her. I'm told that locks of her hair encased in silver sell at a high price in Paris. But this jewel of perfection, with a smile to melt an icy heart and a laugh to soften the most crusty old general, is responding to my rather clumsy attempts to woo her. We have been out dining twice and we have walked out. She holds my hand and she laughs at my jests and stories of adventures in deserts and mountains. In truth, she seems like a girl with me, and myself — well, I am like a brother in some ways but not in most because today we kissed.

June 3

Today was my second hour of joy as a concert-goer, watching her and humming along with a feeling of joy for the rest of the day. She ate with me and we talked for hours about plays and songs and poetry. Irina is teaching me about Shakespeare and I tell her about the tribesmen of the Khyber and the wild horsemen of the Tibetan high plains.

All was happiness and childish play until the late evening when her face changed and a frown put a darkness on her face. She had received a letter from someone, and she was suddenly fearful. I held her and tried to say comforting words, but she would not answer my questions. Nothing I could say could make her reveal the contents of that awful missive.

'All I may tell you, dearest George, is that my family have enemies back in Mother Russia and their evil words and menacing images plant weeds in a bright garden.'

June 4

I am still not able to ride nor even walk freely and so here I am in Tehran, which is in truth a place in Paradise, because Irina is here and she still likes my company. We were at the ambassador's ball tonight and I had to watch her jealously as her dance-card filled up in seconds, as the crowd of male admirers flocked to her. But she smiled at my grumpiness and patted my head like a big sister.

I went late to bed, and was not alone.

June 5

The medical man called today and tutted over my stiff and aching limbs, drawing particular attention to the accursed thigh. There appears to be a possibility that riding may be deuced uncomfortable for some time. He has ordered some more treatment and I have more pills. But of course, she is still here, so joy, say I. After last night I realise that in truth, this is an entirely new sensation with regard to women.

June 6

Damnation be on Fate, the goddess of us all! Irina came this morning, most distracted and perturbed. Her whole manner was one tormented by some gadfly of fear. Even as I held her, those beautiful dark brown eyes flashed, her glance darting to right and left, as if she looked for something threatening her very being. She said that she had to leave for Paris today, with her manager, Glazin, and that she could not confide in me the reason why she was so afraid. She said, 'It is a Russian matter, you need not have any anxiety, George – I will be fine once back in France.'

I determined not to press her further, but made her promise to write to me, and asked that we meet in London as soon as we were able. I gave her a kiss, and on sudden impulse, I gave her my golden brooch, the little owl. 'This is Glaucus, the owl of Minerva,' I said. 'If ever you need me to come to you … at any time … send this to me.' I asked her to vow to do so, and she did. 'But I have Rudolph Glazin to take care of me. He is my cousin, and he is with me everywhere. He will shield me from what happens back home, I'm sure.'

By four in the afternoon she was gone, with Glazin, on board a ship bound for France. No doubt she will be seen and adored on her journey north, across the continent. But I am left alone here with only card-games and dull old history books for amusement.

Harry put down the journal and read no more. He knew his friend as he had never known him before.

———

At Richmond Street, Maria de Bellezza had not failed to avail herself and friends of the company of the celebrities in town, and had invited Irina Danova and Paul Dalevy to her next salon. The world knew Irina, but Monsieur Dalevy, the tenor, was a rising star and little known outside France. At two, Mr Danilo Bruzov was admitted into the parlour, followed by his two singers. In minutes they were ushered into the broad, well-lit room and announced. The cluster of guests clapped politely and Maria began to introduce them to her friends.

'Now everyone, as I promised, we have in the room with us now Mr Bruzov, who is the agent and manager of many famous performers in Europe, and in his care, Miss Irina Danova and Monsieur Dalevy. Mr Bruzov, I rashly promised my friends that we could allow a few questions to your good self and your singers. I hope that is agreeable?'

Both new arrivals were large men. Dalevy was barrel-chested and had a solid, square frame, running to fat even at his young age of thirty. He wore a dark topcoat and shoulder cape and a hat with a wide brim: everything else was a melancholy black and his moustache was waxed and pointed. He did not smile easily, and appeared to be preoccupied, although he was the perfect gentlemanly guest.

Bruzov was an immense man, so broad and solid that he had to make a special effort to turn and address people across the room. He was bald, squat, with a red, pockmarked face, and had to cope with an immense stomach which was held in check by a belt and a cummerbund. Somehow, a waistcoat had been found or made to stretch across his belly. As he spoke, his chin quivered, but his voice was commanding and firm.

'Of course Madame Bellezza, we are here to entertain. Please ask.' He waved an arm across the front of the dozen guests who were all standing in adoration. Most eyes were on Irina, who was stunningly attractive, a woman now of twenty-six, in the full flowering of her beauty, dressed in a skirt of creative lines and ruches, with a white blouse, puff-sleeved and laced on neck and cuffs. The first question was for her.

'Miss Danova, is this your first time in England?'

'Yes indeed, though I have heard much about London, and Mr Bruzov is a new manager. My former manager met with an illness in Paris last week and had to stay there.'

'Do you have friends here?'

There was a short pause, as if she was about to answer but then changed her mind. 'No ..., no. But I soon will have!'

The assembled guests applauded. Maria, who was well aware that her female celebrity was the cause of George's heartache, was by no means merely a hostess. Every party she arranged was also an occasion for gathering information for her contacts in Special Branch, and she had been asked to check on Bruzov. As the big man enjoyed his third brandy, Jemmy Smythe, who was acting as butler for the day, was searching the Russian's greatcoat on the hook in the hall. Jemmy enjoyed playing the role of servant – being the Society's eyes and ears, unobserved, when investigations were being made.

When the party dispersed for the day, and everyone had been invited to the Steinway Hall that night, Smythe reported.

'Nothing definite, Maria, except that I heard the Frenchman say something very odd – that Irina *would do as she was told*. Bruzov has only two days ago taken over as her manager and already he – and apparently the French singer – control her. Why?'

'I wish we knew. But go on.'

'There was also a letter, possibly related to why he is really here.'

'*Really* here?' Maria asked.

'He is possibly a known agent. My information is that a person travelling with Irina was for ten years an officer in the Russian army of the East.'

'The letter merely asked for a meeting but refered to something, not in code but in a very personal phrase. It's "In preparation for Mannheim" – and that's very odd.'

'Why? They're going to the races!'

'Dear me, Maria,' cried the former jockey, 'you need to know the turf a little … the Derby was last June!'

Maria arranged to meet Smythe with the others at the next Oriental dinner, and sat down to try to work out the Mannheim reference. One thing had to be done though: the other Society members needed to be informed of this letter. Of course, they all knew about Lord George's service in the East, and so he was told. But, for the time being, it remained a puzzle.

———

In a small hotel room in Dieppe, Rudolph Glazin was raging, in a sweaty delirium, on the corner bed. He was trying to talk about the London tour. '*We shall have to inform the manager at The Royal Court … that task remains undone, Irina my dear … it remains undone. We have to be … have to be professional!*'

Two men sat by his side. One, with some medical knowledge, answered the nervous questions of the other, who was so agitated that he occasionally started with apprehension, looked closely at Glazin, and then to the other man for reassurance. 'Why has he not gone yet, Piotr?'

'He has a strong heart. Sometimes they fight far more than is natural.'

'You … you gave him the right dose?'

'Of course. Now if you can't handle this, go and get me a coffee. Go!'

The man was only too pleased to go, and when the door closed the other took a pillow and made a gentle, soothing sound, cooing like a mother about to sing a lullaby. 'Oh now, my dear man … now is the time for that eternal rest … your pain will soon leave you.'

He placed the pillow over Glazin's sweat-covered face and forced the weight of his body on top, pressing down with all his force.

'See, my old friend … the darkness comes and you sleep … no more struggling.'

He remained in position for some time, being sure that beneath him there was no struggling, no fighting for perhaps a last intake of precious air. When all was still, he released the pressure and sat back.

A few minutes later the other man came in, carrying a cup of hot coffee. He looked at the bed and then at his accomplice. 'Piotr … he has gone then?'

'Yes. He went quietly in the end.'

———

In the Septimus Club, Lord George was almost ready for the evening at the Steinway Hall. He had been careful to prepare himself so that he looked entirely different from the army officer Irina had first met in Persia. Harry was accompanying him, and the professor was asked more than once if his friend's appearance was suitable.

'Suitable? Why, you are utterly and hopelessly like an adolescent. Still in love with this woman, aren't you?'

George, now on his third whisky and feeling almost bold enough to talk, said, 'Harry, make I speak directly … I mean, from the heart?'

'Well, if you must old boy, but, well, it's most irregular.'

'I don't care one collop of pig's meat if it's irregular. Look, for five years I have tried to forget her. She went home, I went back to the frontier and my duty … the years ate away my feelings, or so I thought until yesterday and that note.'

Harry Lacey's face was bright red. Emotions were something he stayed clear of, and here was a situation calling for the kind of tact he found to be a challenge. Pretending to fuss over his waistcoat buttons, to play for time, he eventually said, 'The point is, if this is what all those romances are about well, then, speak to her … go to her after the concert tonight and express your feelings old man!'

'Do you know, you're talking sense, Harry. The truth is that you *can* talk about matters other than end-rhymes and couplets. You're a scholar *and* a gentleman!'

—·—

At the Steinway Hall in Marylebone Lane, the assembled audience had filled every seat and there was a mood of excitement across the open space as people shuffled with bags and coats, and the crowd whispered their opinions and talked in high praise of Miss Danova. Some recalled that they had seen her in Paris; others marvelled at her Russian beauty. 'She has such a divine Slavic face ... what a dramatic profile!' they cooed, and 'I'm thrilled that she's singing Schubert.' Then all was silent as Bruzov walked onto the stage and bowed.

George and Harry were in some of the best seats at the end of the second row, and, from behind a pillar, Irina squinted to see if she could make out George in the audience. She could – his tall figure and his nobility stood out, at least for her. She smiled. Behind her the words, 'Be ready now, Miss, please!' were snapped out in the French accent she had come to hate.

'Ladies and gentlemen, let us welcome, to first of all sing two songs from Schubert's *Die Winterreise*, Miss Irina Danova!' Bruzov flagged one chunky arm towards her and Irina came on to great applause. As Bruzov walked slowly away from view, she looked around and spoke.

'I will begin with *Gute Nacht*, my personal favourite, which ends with a lover writing "good night" on the gate of his beloved – something I cannot recommend to you in this beautiful city, which should be left unblemished.'

Irina had not the slightest notion that Lord George Lenham-Cawde, who was surrounded by nobility and by the new aristocracy of wealth and so was perfectly aware that he was being constantly scrutinised, felt deep inside him the unsettling disturbances of the bitter-sweet emotions he had known before when in the company of this woman. She had not changed at all, and her allure was more appealing than ever.

George had first had to look at Bruzov, and he hated the sight of him. This fat cur was bullying the object of his affection. Then there was the Mannheim letter, which Lord George was certain now indicated some kind of espionage work in which Bruzov was engaged.

The Schubert songs were finished, and then on came Paul Dalevy to sing two duets with Irina. After loud and long applause, the audience stood and shouted 'bravo' as the singers bowed.

The crowd gradually dispersed into the chilly evening, calling for cabs or walking to parties in Manchester Square or to their hotels around George Street and Wigmore Street. Harry waited by the exit as Lord George walked to the side door, announcing his name to an usher. He was asked if he had been invited backstage. His reply was that he was an old friend of Miss Danova's from years ago. The man was not going to let him in, but Bruzov appeared from behind and when told that it was Lord Lenham-Cawde, he ordered the man to let George in.

Within minutes he was standing in a large sitting room full of armchairs and low tables, at which a gathering of admirers and enthusiasts sat. Irina was sitting in an ornate Georgian chair, with Bruzov to one side, seeming to guard her. The Frenchman was standing behind, not wanting to be a part of proceedings.

'Lord George Lenham-Cawde,' announced a voice from his side as George entered the room. Heads turned and all conversation stopped. Irina looked at him and maintained a professional posture. But Bruzov, always impressed by English status and tradition, rushed across, bowed, and then held out his hand. It was all George could do to prevent himself from striking the fat Russian, but dignity was intact as he shook his hand and found a false smile from somewhere. He walked across to where Irina sat, and bowed to kiss her lace-gloved hand. He had told her, five years earlier, how he adored her hands, which were the hands Goya painted. *'No daintiness, my love, Goya liked the chunky, strong hands, of women who could work.'* He had said this with a laugh, and as he kissed them now, he whispered, 'Like Goya's!' They both smiled, but as hers faded her eyes spoke to him, and they gave a silent appeal for help.

'Miss Danova is very tired. I allowed only fifteen minutes for talk here. I must ask you to leave, ladies and gentlemen,' Bruzov said firmly. As the small group left, George was about to try to speak more familiarly with Irina when Paul Dalevy put his considerable bulk in the way.

'My dear Lord Lenham-Cawde, our prima donna is very tired.'

'I will not tire her any further … I merely wish to speak for a minute.' George raised a hand but two henchmen appeared at his side and Dalevy took Irina by the elbow and led her away into the recess behind.

'Time for supper, My Lord,' one of the henchmen said.

Back at the Septimus Club, Lord George was worried. 'Something is deeply wrong, Harry. She is a virtual prisoner!'

'Well, drinking whiskies at this rate will not help, George. You need a plan.'

'Plan? What the deuce can I do? There's a cabal around her. It's like a fortress of … of very large men!'

'But you're an army man, you must have a plan?' said Harry.

George stood up and paced the room from one side to the other, glancing into the billiard room where the young ones were frittering away time as usual. 'It's no use, Harry, this is a desperate situation. What I need is information. Could we have another afternoon tea arranged by Maria? Or some way of finding out more about this Bruzov man? While I'm at it, what's this Mannheim affair?'

'You have me there old friend. But what we need is Smythe!'

Jemmy Smythe, long the filter of information from Eddie and his colleagues in Special Branch, had been expecting a call from the long lounge, as he sat and studied the form for the York meeting that week. Unusually, he was not called for but was in fact advanced upon by George and Harry, who came hurriedly into the quiet reading room, which was fortunately empty but for Smythe.

'Ah My Lord …' Smythe stood up.

'Oh don't be silly, Smythe. I need information …'

'Well, I'd say Redbank for the York meeting tomorrow, a sound wager at a hundred to seven.'

'You're being obtuse, Smythe … you know why I'm here!'

'Yes. Take a seat and I'll give you a lecture on Russian history My Lord.'

They all huddled in a corner area, heads bowed close as Smythe helped himself to a bowl of sweetmeats which had been left close to hand. 'Now, gentlemen, after Maria's little party the other day I asked Eddie to tell me what is known about these Russians. You will recall that Tsar Alexander was murdered, nine years ago now, as he drove along in St Petersburg, ready for a parade of his worthy soldiers. He was the victim of a party of political radicals called Narodnaia Volia. Two years later, My Lord, you met Miss Danova in Tehran. There is a link. Eddie informs me that, as Russia has not experienced the kind of changes many wish to have happened, there are still many radicals. The girl you met in Persia was the sister of a leading light in a very advanced political group – more advanced in thinking even than the Narodnaia.'

'What? Is she in the hands of the authorities? Why have they not taken her to Russia? Why is she free, and here?' demanded George.

'Please do not be concerned My Lord … we do not know the answer to that question. But we must assume that she is not a target. But she may be … an *instrument*. That is as much as Eddie and his police brains have ascertained.'

'Well, man, they may be here for some nefarious purpose,' said Harry; 'all that Derby Day allusion! Who knows, they may be out to do some evil here!'

'My instinct is that we should find their hotel and drag her out to safety!' George said defiantly, now red with fury.

'Be patient,' soothed Smythe, 'Maria is putting out her spies and Eddie has men following them.'

'I'll try, but it's damned hard!' George shouted out to the world in general.

———

In the Charing Cross hotel, Bruzov and his performers occupied a suite overlooking the river. In one sitting room, Irina and her maid were left to fill their time as they wished, but they were under observation, and Irina could not leave the hotel without permission, and this was restricted to a few hundred yards.

The morning after the concert at the Steinway Hall, Irina, after a restless night, expected some kind of admonishment from Bruzov. Sure enough, at nine, after breakfast, Bruzov entered the room. 'What was all that last night – who is this Lord Lenham-Cawde?'

'I have no idea. He liked me. Men do.'

'My dear Irina, you know very well why we are here. This is not a holiday. Remember what you have to do. There is no time for, how shall I say, attachments. If you know this man, or if he is important in some way, then forget it. I happen to know that he is a sad bachelor, gambling and wasting time at the Septimus Club where these English aristocrats fritter away their lives. Forget him. Do I have to remind you what will happen if we fail?'

'Of course not.'

'Then, as you know, today we do it.'

Irina was left alone with her thoughts, but could think of no way out. Mother Russia would dominate lives, as always. But there was one thing she could do. Bruzov had told her what she wanted to know – where to find George. If George were involved he could be in danger, but she could think of nothing else. She took the little golden owl brooch and kissed it, and then called for her maid.

'Sarah, I know I can trust you. I want you to do something for me … it's very important – a matter of life and death. Do you understand?'

The girl made a little bow. 'Yes Milady. What is it?'

Irina kissed Glaucus and put him in an envelope, addressing it to Lord Lenham-Cawde at the Septimus Club. She used the hotel notepaper, with the letter-head and address.

'I'll make sure it gets there Miss,' said Sarah.

Irina put a sovereign into the girl's palm.

———

As Lord George occupied himself at Maria's residence, Harry had spent the first hours of the day racking his brain, trying to think of a way to help his friend, before finally admitting defeat and picking up *The Times* lying on the table in the club sitting room. He read a feature on his friend Arthur Sullivan, who was apparently planning a new, serious opera. Flicking through the pages, he found the day's events. An announcement caught his attention:

MESMERISM AND SIR FAWLEY JONES

At Buckingham Street, Strand, at 3: the Foreign Secretary, Sir Fawley Jones, whose interest in matters psychical are well known, will be introducing the celebrated practitioner of mesmerism, Jurgen Mannheim. He has been invited by the Society for Psychical Research to demonstrate the powers of hypnotic states in medicine. As Mannheim has written: 'We learn from Mesmerism that there are in all of us hidden reserves of force, physical and moral, and there are vast unexplored tracts in our nature.'

Harry Lacey almost jumped from his seat. What was this? There was Mannheim and there too was the Foreign Secretary. Surely this was more than coincidence. But he needed to know more before he acted, so he determined to go to his files and study the biographical profile of Sir Fawley Jones.

Back at his rooms in Edwardes Square he soon found the file he was looking for and read: 'Jones, Sir Fawley. B. 1848. Served in the East as military attaché in Delhi; later in first intelligence on gazetteer of the northern provinces. Politics – MP, 1880. Foreign Secretary 1882.' Something was taking shape in Harry's mind. Yes, he thought, it was a matter of who is attending and with whom, and why?

Glancing at the wall clock, he saw that it was almost one. There may not be time to cross London to collect George and then go on to the Strand, so he returned to the Septimus Club, wrote a message to be delivered to him at Maria's, and then decided to go immediately to Scotland Yard and inform Eddie that he had found a link between Mannheim and the forthcoming event involving a prominent politician. As he left the Club, the letter arrived for George from Irina, and it was put on a shelf labelled 'L' under the charge of the commissionaire.

———

After leaving Maria's Richmond Street address George decided to walk down the Edgware Road as far as Marble Arch, in order to think. His mind was preoccupied with the dilemma regarding Irina. The fact of the matter, he reflected, was that she was either excessively protected from her public, or that there was some other, more sinister, reason.

Instinct told him that there was something deeply wrong. His mind went back to her troubled face before they parted in Tehran, and how she would not tell him the source of her worries. He raked his memory to try and recall any information she had given him during their time together. She was from St Petersburg and her real name was Polichova, her father being Dmitri Polichevski – some kind of university lecturer. Then, as he stopped to concentrate, he remembered a phrase she had once said: 'My father wants to take away the teeth of the Church.' She had referred to the Church more than once, and the local power-hungry officials.

Have I found myself in love with a dangerous radical? he asked himself. Noticing that he was now at the corner of George Street, he decided to see if Harry was at home.

Harry's neighbour saw him knocking and said that he had seen the professor going out a short while ago. There was nothing for it but to take a cab to the Septimus Club.

———

In the second-floor room at Buckingham Street thirty people were gathered, eagerly awaiting the appearance of Jurgen Mannheim. The group included scientists, medical men, rationalists of all hues, some believers in thought-reading and a cluster of keen members of the Society for Psychical Research, who were apt to delight in any kind of experiment or demonstration whatsoever which might introduce an element of mystery.

There were three reserved seats at the back of the well-lit room, and at ten to three, heads turned to see Irina Danova, accompanied by two stocky, solid guardians. There was a sudden increase in noise as the conversation level lifted and many spoke the name 'Danova'. Monsieur Dalevy and Bruzov struggled to find a degree of comfort, and an attendant tactfully brought in a large chair for the big Russian, who sweated and puffed after climbing the stairs, and patted his face with a gaudy handkerchief.

But Irina was disturbed by some new knowledge. As she had stepped into the cab on the way, she heard Monsieur Dalevy say to Bruzov, 'Don't worry, we took care of Glazin'. She wanted to scream and lunge at the Frenchman. Her cousin and former manager, Rudolph, was supposed to be ill and resting in Paris. Her heart was beating so fast that she feared a collapse. These men, they had killed her friend, and now they were pushing her to help in the ruin of another man.

Yet she somehow contained her passion and as they took their seats, she longed for George to come. Only he could save her. Then Monsieur Dalevy whispered in her ear, 'Now remember, my dear, Sir Fawley Jones is our man. You are to take him outside to the stairs when things stop and people are having drinks … then leave the rest to me.'

She nodded. All she had been told was that Sir Fawley Jones caused many deaths, many years ago, in India. If she did not play her part, her father would die. The simple balance of facts was enough to give her the resolve she needed. But now things were different. Now *they* were the killers.

———

Shortly before three o'clock George was at the Septimus Club and had collected his letter. He opened it immediately and the little golden owl fell into his hand. The note wrapped around it read: '19, Buckingham Street – come quickly.' He was in a cab within a minute, shouting out the address. The cabby did his best but there was a throng of people, horses and carts, packing every street and progress was slow. He rapped on the roof, and heard the shout of, 'Tryin' me best, Guv. Some wagon fell over on the 'aymarket … I'll turn and try another way!'

———

Harry and Eddie had made it to Buckingham Street, entering the premises by a back staircase. Eddie told the attendant who he was, and they were allowed to wait outside the room, behind the speakers.

'I've had no time to tell Sir Fawley Jones,' Eddie said. 'He needs to know that there may be danger.' But before he could intervene, Sir Fawley Jones stood up and introduced Jurgen Mannheim. The Foreign Secretary was a man of military bearing: upright, firm-jawed and well built. He spoke with a balance of information and speculation, showing a deep interest in things paranormal.

'Some of my colleagues in the House were rather tormenting me for coming here today, such are the limits of their poor benighted minds. But I feel sure that our guest will provoke some thought here today. I present Jurgen Mannheim, mesmerist.'

After some applause, Mannheim began his talk, and after an explanation of his life and his intentions with this 'new science' he asked for someone from the audience to be his aide in demonstrating the hypnotic state.

A young man volunteered and was asked about any illness he might have. He replied, 'I have a st ... stutter you s ... see Herr M ... M ... Mannheim.'

A few people tried unsuccessfully to suppress their giggles of amusement and they received a hard stare from Sir Fawley Jones.

'You have had treatment for this I assume?' Mannheim asked.

'Everything has failed, Sir. A dozen medical men have tried to remove the stutter, and they have failed.'

'Very well, let us begin.' The young man sat before Mannheim, who proceeded to swing a pendant before him and speak in a soothing, lyrical way. He told the young man that he would speak fluently, with no hesitation, and he suggested some little tricks to use, in his mind, to feel the courage to speak.

The result was impressive, and the patient proceeded to answer questions about his life from the audience with complete confidence and without hesitation. There was widespread applause and many eager questions. Sir Fawley Jones then invited everyone for drinks in the adjoining room.

With Monsieur Dalevy's hand on her arm, Irina was urged forward from the back of the room. 'Now,' he hissed. 'Go now!' She glanced down and saw a revolver in his hand, half hidden by his cuff. She knew at once what he intended to do and, walking towards Sir Fawley Jones, who saw her and smiled, holding out a hand to greet her, she pointed back to the Frenchman and screamed out, 'He is here to kill you Sir!'

At that moment, George had rushed up the stairs and was pushing his way through the crowd towards Irina. Harry, watching behind, ran and did his best rugby tackle on Sir Fawley Jones, knocking him out of the line of fire. The first bullet hit Irina in the head and she fell instantly, a few feet from George.

The crowd ran for cover, then a crack whipped across the room and the gunman fell to the ground. Eddie had seen that there was no time to allow any advantage to be given to this desperate man.

Eddie ordered everyone away from the dying man, but Sir Fawley Jones had to know who had wanted to take his life. He peered over the man, then said, 'Ah, Kaspari! After all these years … you never forgot.'

'This is Paul Dalevy, the French singer, Sir,' Eddie corrected him.

'No my friend, this is Dmitri Kaspari, of the Russian Army.'

'You will pay in Hell, Jones!' were the dying man's last words.

———

Across the room, George was holding Irina's hand. Now there was nothing and he would never be the same man again. She was cold and still; there was no response to the call of her name and he resigned himself to losing her, lowering his head to kiss her lips one last time.

Another Jack

His chin slammed against the hard wood of the floor and he felt a fist beating at his back. Then the strong hand held him firm. He had no strength to move and could only scream his protest in fitful bursts of strength which he willed from the depths of his misery. Would this animal never stop? The cries turned to sobs. He felt his naked stomach scrape along the wood and something sharp pressed into his belly, as if he were dragged along a bed of nails.

'Please … stop! For pity's sake.'

'Ah soldier boy … my soldier boy … lovely young flesh you have, son…'

His tormentor jabbed at him with his heels, drawing blood-spots where the metal had bitten.

'Oh you beautiful little fanny. But why so still?' The man slammed his fist into the floor.

The brother and sister were in their early twenties and had had a good night out. They were on their way home to their lodging house when they decided to turn into Eldon Street and pay a call on their younger brother.

'Well, he never leaves the home as far as I can see, Jess,' said Charlie with a wry tone.

'No, he'll be working on the next great historical canvas I expect,' Jessie laughed.

They knocked with some force, as he was on the second floor and always had his door shut. But the front door swung open and with exclamations of surprise they went in, Charlie leading the way, shouting, 'Willy … it's Charlie. You there?'

'He's probably dreaming of ancient Rome!' Jessie smirked. The door to the artist's room was open as well, and Charlie went straight in, noticing the clothes strewn across the floor and a corner table knocked over. The place was silent and, feeling alarmed, Charlie told his sister to stay back and wait.

'Is something wrong?'

Focusing his eyes in the gloom, with only moonlight to guide him, Charlie saw a heap of canvases piled up high in the corner and he moved towards them. Moving two or three out of the way, he saw part of an arm. He took the last ones away and saw his brother lying on the floor, completely naked, arms spread wide, his head turned to one side. 'Willy … for God's sake, Willy!' he shouted. But there was no movement, and when he put a hand to his brother's head, there was the sticky, matted mess of blood.

'Stay back, Jess … stay back!'

But it was too late. Jessie was standing behind him and she flung herself down across her brother, sobbing, wanting him to live. Charlie felt for a pulse. 'He's gone …'

Detective Inspector Edward Carney of Scotland Yard appeared at the scene shortly after the police surgeon, who had come from the station on Hyde Park. A constable was at the gate and he told Eddie that the brother and sister of the dead man were with a lady on the ground floor, being comforted. 'Sergeant Duff's up there Sir, with the Doc.'

As he entered the room, he heard the sergeant ask, 'Was he successful then, this William Dockray?'

Eddie answered before the doctor could. 'Yes, very. He has RA after his name, Sergeant Duff.'

'Oh, good day Sir.' Duff turned to greet the Detective Inspector and moved to one side.

'What facts do we have, doctor?' Eddie asked, turning to the police surgeon.

'Well, Carney, the poor man was cracked from behind with a hard object – a hammer, or a tool of some kind. You've heard of him then?'

'Yes, comes of mixing with some literary gents I know. Mr Dockray was one of the most promising young artists of our time, I believe.'

'Hmm. Now, I've had a close look. As you see, he is naked and was found that way. But the strangest thing, Carney, is here … see these pricks here, on his side? They're on the other side too.'

'What are they – spur marks? As if he was being *ridden*?'

'Exactly. Therefore we have to conclude that he was not simply killed, by a burglar for instance, who wanted him out and quick, but by someone who tormented him, played with him, shall we say.'

'A maniac then, Sir?' It was the constable from downstairs.

'Who are you, constable?' asked Carney, frowning.

'PC Telfer, Sir.'

Eddie nodded and walked around the room. 'Has anything been moved?'

'Well Sir,' the constable continued, 'the brother downstairs says he took a lot of paintings off the body. I was the first officer here Sir, as I was on Victoria Road, round the corner, when the lady shouted for me. His brother and sister was weeping over him.'

'It's a hellish mess …' Eddie said, striding around, taking in all the detail. 'So this brother threw all the paintings over there, constable?'

'No, I piled 'em there Sir. They was in a right mess. That last one is grim … I seen the name on it, GWR – like the bloomin' railway Sir!' He laughed, but stopped when he saw Eddie's serious stare. Eddie noticed that the young officer had some teeth missing at the front and he covered them as he laughed.

'Yes, grim indeed … some kind of scene depicting a man with a face almost deathly! Hardly a portrait anyone would want.'

Eddie asked for the doctor's notes and copied the salient points into his own notebook. He then went downstairs to talk to the brother and sister, who sat with a woman who gave her name as Mary Medd.

'I lives here Sir … knew Mr Dockray a little bit, though he kept to himself. He would be painting day and night, he would, said to me once that he had to make a name, be the best portrait painter in London! That's what he said. I'll make you a cup o' tea shall I Sir?'

Eddie thanked her and turned his attention to the two people on the sofa. The brother remained silent, but the girl said, 'I'm Jessie. Willy was the youngest, and he lived alone, but we're not far away, though we didn't see him often.' She started to sob again and her brother held her.

The tea arrived. 'It's nice and sweet Sir … here.' The others declined. Eddie sipped the hot liquid and watched them, then asked the obvious question: 'Do you know if your brother had any enemies? Any professional enemies, perhaps? Was anyone jealous of his success?'

Charlie spoke for the first time: 'No, officer, not at all. He was the friendliest, most affectionate person … no one hated him, I would swear to that.'

'But you saw little of him, so you're guessing?'

'Well, I suppose … but I know … I mean, I *knew* my own brother.'

'Very well. The constable has your address so I'll perhaps speak to you again. Thanks for the tea, Mrs Medd.'

'Pleasure, Sir,' she said, before continuing. 'He was quiet, but had friends … oh yes, I mean, only last week there was that soldier round. You know, Sir, he was lonely. Terrible thing, loneliness. The city's full of lonely people … only there's nobody to 'elp. No doctors for it, like.'

'Soldier?'

'Why yes, he told me once he liked to paint military men. I s'pose the soldier was a model … they get paid don't they? Gives 'em a bit of drinking money, I would say.'

'Did he have many soldiers round to visit, Mrs Medd?'

'I couldn't say … but there was another … some time a few months back. I asked him who he was painting, you know. Whether he liked painting soldiers. I mean, stands to reason don't it? All that colour, that brass and shine! Everybody likes to look at soldiers marching and that.'

A story was forming in Eddie's mind. It was a story in which a lonely young artist was the protagonist.

———

At the police station on Hyde Park, part of A Division, Sergeant Duff, near retirement, settled at his desk and grunted at the pile of mail handed to him from his duty constable. Duff had had enough of police work: after twenty years on the streets, and before that a stretch in the army out in India, he was looking forward to some time growing potatoes. He was thinking this as he opened each letter, glanced at it and then opened another. Some were the usual – complaints about the dangers of Hyde Park at dusk. These middle-class upright types, they moaned all the time about drunks and people generally having a lark.

But then he saw something different. It was a letter written in red ink and in capital letters, and it brought a shiver to his body, as it immediately made him think of Whitechapel just two years back. 'Constable,' he hollered, 'get Detective Carney *right now*!'

Carney was shouted for, and he came quickly, and he and Duff studied the words together in silence:

TO CARNEY, OLD CHARMER

I'M RIDDING THE WORLD OF POUFS, LIKE THAT ATIST

DEJENERITS WILL DOOM US ALL

JACK THE JOCKEY

'Oh no, please, not again! It's a Bedlam case, surely, Mr Duff?' said Eddie.

Duff shook his head and his double chin wobbled. 'He knows about the painter, Sir. It's not been in the press yet.'

Carney was troubled. He took a few steps towards the window. From here he could see the Knightsbridge barracks. 'Time for me to take a walk over there, Mr Duff. Could you have a note taken to the Septimus Club, please?' He wrote a short message to Harry Lacey.

At the barracks Carney asked to see the Commanding Officer and he was shown by the orderly to the officer's room. As they walked along a long corridor, the orderly – a short, upright man, with a full moustache and greased hair parted down the middle – spoke abruptly. 'You're a detective Sir?'

'Yes, based just over the park here.'

'Hope some of the boys have not been thievin' again Sir. It's beneath a soldier to steal.'

'Indeed, Mr, er …'

'Corporal Dignan Sir, 3rd Battalion Grenadiers. Just back from Sudan, Sir.'

'Oh, dangerous.'

'Was for General Gordon, Sir. We let him down greatly. He was a saint, Sir. Now here's Colonel Dacre.' He opened a door, took a step forward, saluted, and announced Inspector Carney.

The colonel stood up from behind his desk and shook hands with Eddie. 'Take a seat Inspector. I think I know why you're here … the incident the other night … the men can be on rather a short fuse when they're back from active service.'

He was youthful for a senior officer, moving animatedly, flapping his arms and making grand gestures.

'No, it's not about any drunken business Sir …' Eddie said, sitting back in a chair and folding his greatcoat over one knee. 'I want to ask you about something rather delicate. You will be reading about a murder in the evening paper, Sir, and I have to tell you, in confidence, that the suspect may be a trooper.'

'Now, Inspector Carney, as you are fully aware, these impressive new barracks, they are not simply stone and mortar of the best quality … no, they are composed of flesh and blood as well, the cream of the British bloodstock in fact! Our men are the best. They may be involved in trivial scuffles from time to time, but they are not murderers …'

'I always understood that you military men were … well, paid to kill.'

'Ah, you're being light and easy with me, Inspector. You know very well what I mean.'

'The fact remains that soldiers have been seen on more than one occasion visiting the house where a young artist was murdered, just a short walk from here. Consequently I have to have a certain level of suspicion.'

The colonel sat back and pressed his palms together. Eddie thought he was repressing an angry reaction. 'Inspector Carney, my men pay visits to civilians on all kinds of occasions. Surely this artist chap had lots of other visitors?'

'There were certain details at the crime scene which lead us to believe that the killer may have been a horseman.'

'Hah! There you are … the park is streaming with people on horseback. My battalion is a cavalry one, yes, but they are surrounded by horsemen all the time! You appear to have no real evidence, Inspector Carney. Now, I do have rather a lot of paperwork to do …'

'Very well. I'll show myself out. But I may return with more questions.'

The colonel stood up and gave a curt bow. 'Of course.'

On the way out, Corporal Dignan stood to attention and then asked, 'Any progress, Sir? There are some poor excuses for humanity about the park at night, of course ... not all men in uniform.'

'Quite,' said Eddie, and walked away, full of thought.

———

That night as Eddie walked into the Septimus Club to meet Harry, half a mile away on the edge of the Serpentine a young man was staring into the water as dusk invaded the early evening. He was muttering to himself but looked up when a movement caught his eye. A tall soldier in a red coat stood next to him. 'Oh, good evening. Very quiet tonight,' he murmured.

'Yes, I was enjoying a cool walk, as, I see, were you.'

'Yes, I was talking to myself ... sorry about that. I'm quite sane. Merely thinking of a poem.'

The soldier came nearer. 'Ah, a poet! I never met one before, but in the army, of course, a poet is of singular value ... when it comes to writing home to loved ones, I mean.'

'Oh, I see.'

The soldier slipped his arm through the young man's and beamed at him. 'Well, young poet, would you like some company?'

The poet nodded and patted the soldier's hand, then they walked into the falling darkness.

—–—

'Here's the note, Harry. I'm hoping it's a damned idiot with a frenzied imagination,' Eddie said, as he sat with Harry Lacey in the library at the Septimus Club. But matters were awkward: Harry was seemingly in considerable pain. He moved slightly and grimaced as if something was stabbing him.

'Now Harry old friend, are you ill?'

'Oh damn the thing!' said the Professor. 'It's a little personal, Eddie. I'm at war with my extending paunch, as you know … and, well, the truth is, I'm wearing the new Rossiter Manform Retainer.'

'The what?'

'It's a kind of corset that holds in any excess rotundity. It's hellish. Whalebone and steel, I think. I'm struggling to breathe.'

'Harry, here I am with a new Ripper to deal with and you're, well, having female problems!' He couldn't resist jabbing his friend in the ribs, causing yet another moan of pain.

'I shall persevere – it does trim the figure somewhat, you have to agree,' winced Harry.

'Yes, right, well gather yourself and read this.'

Harry screwed up his eyes and adjusted his pince-nez. It took him a while to register what he had read. 'Oh really! This is surely some childish prank! You must have received a multitude of these letters since Jack?'

Eddie frowned. 'The thing is, Harry, the man who wrote this *knew* of the death of William Dockray.'

'Ah yes … here's the report in today's *Times*. Clearly you told them very little. Most of the piece is about the real Jack, terrifying the populace.'

'What I want is Professor Lacey the critic's report on this please – some thoughts from the student of language!'

Harry scratched his nose and then pulled his professional face, the one he put on when discussing the themes of Shakespeare's late plays. 'First, this spelling is surely false – artificial. This infantile mind is trying to echo Jack himself. He's read the Jack letters in the press, and he's teasing you rather. My intuition tells me that he's well educated and is revelling in this guise.'

Eddie blew his nose. He had a cold coming on and his head throbbed. 'Harry, that's very impressive, in spite of your Rossiter!'

'Leave it with me,' said Harry. 'I'll get into my files and report back, perhaps write you a response after I've had more time to think.'

The Detective Inspector was glad to get home to his comfortable chair and his wife's tender care.

———

The next morning, the landlady of Reston Buildings, Queens Gate, took a poached egg up to her young lodger. She tapped on the door and walked in; what she saw was enough to make her start and the tray and its contents flew into the air. Staring at her from the floor was the dead face of her lodger, who was lying naked on the carpet.

When Carney arrived he had plenty of questions for the landlady.

'What did he do, the deceased?' he asked.

'He was a writer, Sir. Poetry ... and I think he wrote a novel too, just came out last month. He had a good many friends – writers, I mean.'

'Had anybody been with him last night?'

'Yes, there was someone, but I only heard them go out. I heard the outside door shut ... about eleven it was. I never disturbed him when he had any friends up there with him.'

'Madam, I'd like to know if he had any military friends? Did you see any soldiers here?'

'Soldiers? I don't know ... it's difficult you see, Sir, as I let him answer the door and let his friends in. He used to tell me when they was expected, so I kept out of the way. I think he liked to be thought independent.'

'How do you mean?'

She smiled. 'Well, I think I mothered him a bit ... made him feel like a child I reckon. Once I was a bit too strong on the mothering bit when he had this editor round, and we had words ... but I understood. He was a grown man after all.'

Eddie thanked her and took a walk around the area. At the end of the street he could see Hyde Park, and he thought again of the barracks. Someone had been there, and had left quite late.

Later that day, Eddie met Harry at the Copper Pot coffee house near the Yard. Harry had been busy with his files and with his own enquiries. He saw that Eddie had a heavy cold and plied him with hot coffee and a shot of whisky. It was a noisy place, but they were used to talking in the hubbub of the city.

'Harry, the pathologist tells me that the weapon used in both killings was a hammer. There was a parallel red mark on one shoulder, and that, he tells me, was almost certainly made by a claw hammer.'

'We're dealing with a madman – this man enjoys taking life … he doesn't rush it.'

Before they could say any more a young man approached. 'Why, Mr Dockray,' said Eddie, surprised. 'You wish to see me?'

'Yes, I went to Scotland Yard and asked for you. They sent me here. I've come about my brother's death.'

'Please, do sit down with us. Harry, this is Charlie, William Dockray's brother. Charlie, this is Professor Lacey.' Charlie nodded at Harry and found room to sit down at the table.

'I was very sorry to hear about your brother's death. I too have lost siblings,' said the professor.

Charlie looked down at his hands, then gathered himself and addressed Eddie. 'Inspector, Jess and I have been talking … and we brought to mind Godfrey Russell. He's a painter and is … was a close friend of Willy's. In fact, we all know him, and we spent time together … trips up the Thames or to the theatre, you know. He's a colourful character.'

'Colourful?' Eddie enquired.

'Inspector, he's an aesthetic type, you know.'

'Walks around with a lily, ready to faint at the sight of beauty?' smiled Harry.

'Not far off the truth. He is thirty-five … never married.'

'He's a gentleman who likes the company of other men … artists, writers, that kind of person?' Eddie was tactful.

'I think I know what you're suggesting, Inspector. Perhaps you are right. Anyway, the point is, we recalled that he and Willy had rowed recently.'

'Rowed? About what?'

'Something about Willy having an exhibition. The thing is, Godfrey, well, he's not exactly successful.'

'And your brother was a member of the Royal Academy, of course,' said Eddie.

'Yes, quite. There was a degree of envy, though I'm not saying that Godfrey could have … you know. We simply felt that you should know.'

'Yes, indeed. Thank you for the information. I will need Mr Russell's address.'

'Ah, now, Inspector … please say you're not going to charge him.'

'No, no. We simply have to cover every line of enquiry.'

'Very well; it's number two, Redcliffe Square, Brompton. I must ask you not to mention my name, or my sister's.'

'Of course. We policemen rarely say more than we have to.'

Charlie Dockray left and Harry, ordering a second muffin and pot of coffee, reported one more item of interest. 'I checked in all my reference material, Eddie. There was something ... merely a paragraph – our Mr Dockray was assaulted. He was involved in a confrontation in Hyde Park, but it never led to any police involvement. Apparently, a writer for the *Morning Chronicle* saw a scuffle and wrote a report. His editor obviously cut it down to a snippet. The Yard would have no records, of course.'

Before anything else was said, a constable rushed in through the doorway and handed Eddie a note. 'It's him, Sir. Thought you needed to see it sharpish.'

'Thank you Iveson. You can get back to the desk. Yes, here we are. It's our man, Harry.' He handed the note to Harry, who was tucking into the muffin. It read:

INSPECTOR CARNEY, SCOTLAND YARD.

THERE GOES NUMBER TWO LADYBOY.

GET BUSY SON. NEXT I'M HAMMERING A BANDSMAN

JACK THE JOCKEY

'Hmm. Interesting,' said Harry. 'No spelling errors this time. I'm quite sure this man is well educated – and he writes '*son*'. That almost certainly means that he is young, and is trying to hint that he is older than you, would you say?'

'Perhaps. He has also given us a clue – he's challenging me. But I have to visit Mr Russell. Will you help later, Harry? I need someone to attempt a delicate task, and you have the man-of-the-world neck to do it.'

'I'll try.'

'We will have to bend the law a little. You need to play the part of a medical chap ... and you have to visit Colonel Dacre at Knightbridge barracks. I'll write down instructions.' He took his notebook and wrote some guidance for the task. Harry took it, read it through and laughed. 'Oh what fun! I always meant to be on the stage, you know. Fancy asking me to investigate degenerates!'

'What did you say – degenerates?'

'Why yes, they're all talking about it in Cambridge ... a new book, but it's in German. The title translates as *Degeneration*. There have been pieces in the papers and journals. It's all about how the human race is going down, old man. We're sinking, morally! Gives us something to talk about in the Senior Common Room. Written by a man called Nordau.'

'Harry, the first "Jack" letter had that word.'

'Why bless my soul, so it did!'

'Our jockey is very up to date. He reads and he thinks indeed. Enjoy your little play-acting!'

Harry turned, a twinge of pain reminding him of the Rossiter Manform Retainer.

Godfrey Russell was writing dinner invitations to his friends in the Atelier Society when his maid announced, 'Detective Inspector Carney for you Sir' and showed Eddie in.

Russell was elegantly dressed, wearing an old-fashioned frockcoat with a rose in the lapel. His moustache was spiked and waxed, and his raven hair fell to his shoulders. His bright blue eyes sparkled, and the smile on his face welcomed Eddie into his cluttered sitting room.

'Detective! What on earth brings the law into my little artist's den? Have I transgressed in some way?' He held out a hand and Eddie shook it before taking a seat on the opposite side of the desk to Russell.

'You find me writing invitations ... I'm celebrating the completion of that portrait over there.' The artist pointed to a painting, held on a very large easel. 'Come and have a closer look, tell me what you think.'

'I'm not exactly well-informed about art, Mr Russell, but I'll gladly take a look.' Eddie walked across and scrutinized the picture, Russell standing behind him. It was completely familiar, showing a white, almost cadaverous face of a young man, leaning with his elbow on a side-table, a large open collar to his shirt and a glass of wine in hand. There, at the bottom, was the signature, 'GWR'.

'Ah, Mr Russell, I have seen one of your paintings before, but not in a gallery. No, it was over the face of a dead man, and that is why I am here.'

Russell put a hand over his mouth and gasped. 'Oh, of course, yes, I understand your reference. My dear friend Willy Dockray. I suppose I've been expecting you.'

'Why?'

'Well, I suppose you question everyone who knows the victim, do you not?'

Eddie nodded, then turned and looked around the room. 'You are very prolific. There must be twenty paintings here.'

'I've been an artist for thirty years, Inspector. I'm now almost fifty. My young friend Willy was just as busy.'

'Yes, and I believe he was RA – is that right?'

'Indeed, unlike myself; my work never seemed to please the Academy panel.'

His smile dropped and there was a frown. 'Ah, I see … you have heard things. No doubt you have been talking to some who knew us … Willy and I.'

'I have. But I deal in facts, nothing else. A detective has no time to let his imagination run riot.'

'No, of course not. Whereas I have to allow the imagination utter freedom. But there is not an inch of hatred in me for Willy, though it must be said he was a fortunate young man. The world liked him. His face was always welcome, whereas I have to work hard simply to be remembered. I'm that strange man who does the pallid faces! That's what the art world says.'

'They think you have but one talent?'

'Exactly. But they all come to my parties.' He laughed. The smile returned. He offered Eddie a glass of wine, but it was refused. Russell walked around, looking at his pictures, and said, 'What care I? It's the work that matters ... posterity too. I'll be known after my death, I'm sure.'

'Indeed. Now I have to ask about the painting found placed on Mr Dockray's face.'

'On his face ... was it damaged?' he asked instinctively, then realised how crass the question must seem and added, 'I only ask because it was a portrait of him. It was a special gift for his twenty-seventh birthday.'

'A portrait of him? Mr Russell, it was nothing like him, surely?' Eddie was puzzled.

'Ah, here I must explain that my portraits are not naturalistic. They deliver a vision.'

Eddie pretended to understand and changed the subject. 'Mr Russell, I have to speak with tact and confidentiality. I must ask you a question regarding Mr Dockray's sexuality.'

Russell positively beamed. He appeared to delight in Eddie's struggle to introduce the subject. His reply was disarmingly direct.

'Inspector, he was what your man in the street calls a *pouf*, as I am. But if you are moving towards asking about sodomitic assignations, then the answer is no. We are discreet, my friends and I, knowing full well the illegality of any such habits.'

'Well, er, yes. Thank you for your candid response Mr Russell. Before I go, I have to ask about the nature of your relationship with Mr Dockray ... I mean, simply your friendship, your attitudes to each other ... I'm not putting this well. I'm asking if you *got on?*'

'Got on? Oh, we had our differences. At times he lost his temper with me … I'm a dogmatic person, Inspector, and I have strong views on art. Being older and more of the world, I tended to comment and give advice.'

'You were a sort of father figure?'

'Good Lord no!' Russell guffawed. 'I wanted to be a big brother, I suppose.'

'Mr Russell, are you able to explain why your portrait of William Dockray was placed over his face – the first one put there, with others piled on top?'

Russell was nonplussed. 'Well, I mean, devil take it, I don't know. Are you implying that someone … the killer … did this?'

'Mr Russell, I'm simply wondering if perhaps you had a row?'

'Ah, I see. You envisage my good self in a murderous rage, hating Willy for rejecting my wonderful painting, then cracking it over his head, frame and all, before I battered him to death.'

'Of course not. But your reply tells me a great deal.'

'What? What! I was being facetious … I was being ironic!'

Eddie thanked Russell for his time and left, with the usual reminder that he might want to speak to him again. It was always a productive little ruse to leave them hanging, uncertain, after an interview.

Days passed and inquiries were made by a number of officers, but none were so bold as Harry Lacey's approach to Colonel Dacre, who thought his officers were listening to 'Professor Golightley', a statistician. The colonel had gathered a dozen officers, some orderlies and ADC's to listen to the professor's study. Harry had worked everything out thoughtfully, and he was in fact in his natural role – lecturing. He stood at a table in the Officers' Mess, the men were at tables, legs crossed and cigarettes in hand, listening with either curiosity or boredom, he was not sure which.

Harry looked absolutely the image of an academic gentleman of the new breed of fact-dominated thinking. He relished the challenge of stepping into the part, and was so convincing that the colonel began to think that he ought to have educative talks more often. Harry warmed to his task.

'Gentlemen, I hope you begin to see my purpose. We live in an age of great scientific progress. Just as your rifles and cannon and guns are being advanced every day, so the science of statistical calculation is advancing, and, in my case, I am compiling facts to help counteract the criminal activities of our day. In short, I need to understand certain social habits, tendencies if you like, of our servicemen.'

Colonel Dacre's orderly, Corporal Dignan, asked permission to speak.

'Of course ... you have a question?'

'What specific facts do you require, Sir?'

'My special interest is in those military men who deviate from normal behaviour in matters of sexual preference.' There was muttering and someone swore. But Dignan was quick to respond. 'You mean the pretty-boys? May I speak freely?' He looked around the room and received nods and encouraging noises. 'Now, army men know that having carnal relations is a necessary part of soldiering. It deals with the … the natural, or sometimes unnatural physical needs, as you might say … of men with red-blooded … er, promptings of nature. Now, we are fully aware of the law, and that sodomites get a lash and time inside *etcetera etcetera* … but even in the Guards we have some human understanding.'

'Rot man … what have you been reading?' an officer behind the speaker retorted. 'Professor, you can put in your statistical tables that there are no poufs in the Grenadier Guards. We would drum them out, right?'

There were murmurs of approval.

'Very well, so of the four hundred men at present here, there are no coves with any deviant behaviour with regard to their, er, carnal desires?'

'Well we did have that Welshman and his ruddy penchant for goats! The regimental mascots had to wear chastity belts!' The joker provoked general laughter. At this the colonel got to his feet and declared the meeting over. The men filed out, some giving a hard stare in the direction of the professor, leaving him with the colonel and Corporal Dignan.

The colonel was already somewhat upset, having had a visit from three police constables all wanting to speak with the musicians in his battalion, as Eddie had sent a messenger to the Yard to get busy responding to Jack's challenge.

'Professor Golightley,' said the colonel, 'what exactly do you statistics chaps do with your facts?'

'Well, we produce tabular information ... percentages, columns, charts, that sort of thing. For instance, you may care to know that between 1880 and 1883 the City of London Police had a conviction rate of thirty-four per cent.' Harry had made that up. The 'fact' interested Dignan. 'Disgusting Sir,' he said. 'There is no wonder that the human race is thinning out, going bad ... I mean, these infidels, like the savages what topped General Gordon, God rest his soul, they are not human but beasts, below the human.'

Harry was intrigued by this comment, and couldn't help thinking about Nordau and his new book. 'Corporal Dignan, can you read German?' he asked.

The two military men looked at each other, puzzled. 'What the deuce has that to do with anything Professor?' the colonel asked.

'Oh merely an academic interest.'

'The answer is no, Sir. English is the finest tongue in the world and there is no cause to acquire another.' Dignan's answer seemed to please his superior. It was the ideal moment for Harry to leave, and as he walked across Hyde Park, he had a feeling that Dignan was lying.

Eddie, full of cold and feeling decidedly ill, decided not to go back to the Yard after his meeting with Russell. He had set things in motion protecting every army bandsman who could be located at Hyde Park, and he needed to think. The painting by Russell had been slammed over the dead man's head with some considerable force. There was venom there. Not something that would happen in the course of a slight altercation between friends.

It was only a few minutes' walk from the Strand by Charing Cross, to Bow Street, E Division. He strolled up towards Maiden Lane, then onto the edge of Covent Garden, where he made straight for the stalls of cut flowers, one of his greatest delights in the city in which he had grown up. The noise of the streets faded when people walked into this rich array of colour: there were roses, carnations and all hues of wallflowers. He lingered a while to take in the wonderful buildings; one place was very special: the church of St Paul's. His grandfather's best friend, Thomas Rowlandson, was buried there; Thomas had made a name for himself as an artist, but had been a terrible gambler, losing everything he had at the table, and then working all hours in his studio to earn more funds. Such was the precarious nature of men's lives.

His meditation was cut short when a voice to his side said, 'Good day to you, Inspector … Detective, in fact!'

It was his old friend, Sergeant Alfred Taylor, jolly as always. The two men shook hands and the sergeant beamed. The sergeant was an old friend whom Eddie had known for many years.

'Hello Alf! I heard you were retiring come Christmas?'

'Yes indeed; come, let us walk along to the station – I have to be back.'

Bow Street, the famous police station and court, was around the corner, and they were soon standing by Sergeant Taylor's high desk in the reception foyer, with a crowd milling around. The hubbub subsided as a constable ushered some noisy costermongers outside, and as Taylor took out a duty sheet with a list of names, Eddie gave an account of his life 'across town', as he put it. 'Yes, I deal with some high and mighty sorts … not quite the same level of villain as you and I were used to Alf.'

'Aye … still doing the same paperwork … see this? You used to write these!' He held up the sheet and Eddie read down, his eye resting on the name 'Telfer'.

'Hey, Alf … you have a Constable Telfer. That's not such a common name is it?'

'Honestly Eddie, your brain never stops questioning…'

'Well, it's just that there's a Telfer at A Division … maybe they're brothers?'

Sergeant Taylor thought for a moment. 'Our Telfer … he's a young man …'

Eddie couldn't resist pressing his friend for a little more detail. It was habit with him. 'Your Telfer, has he got all his teeth?'

'As a matter of fact, no. He was in a fight about a month back – had his two front teeth knocked out by some drunk. Course, this list is last night's. He's off duty tonight.'

'Can I have his address?'

'Of course ... just a minute.' The sergeant went into an office and there was the sound of shuffling paper, then he came back with an address written on a sheet of note paper.

'Alf, I know it's been a long time,' said Eddie, 'and I'm really sorry, but you just gave me something I have to fasten onto like a mastiff, right now, my friend. I promise you'll get the pint of porter I had in mind, soon as.'

———

October nights were turning chilly and the darkness came early now. Not so many revellers were out at night to take the air. On the edge of Hyde Park a group of young guardsmen were out for a drink or two. They had gone out in numbers, after sobering words from a police sergeant about a killer in the area. But not all soldiers had been around when the police called, and one of these was a young cornet player, and he was alone.

He hoped that the night would not be a disappointing one, that Charles would come as he said he would. They had agreed to meet at the Achilles statue, and as the trooper reached the giant figure he waited, filling in time by looking up at the colossal figure of the Greek hero, with sword and shield.

Behind him someone said, 'Cost ten thousand pounds that ... way back in 1822. I understand that the ladies of the land paid for it, in honour of the great Duke of Wellington himself.'

The young trooper spun round. 'You came, Charles! And by God, you're a soldier too!'

His friend was wearing the red coat, striped trousers and white gauntlets of a private soldier.

'You never said you were in the army! What regiment?'

'I'm wearing the clobber of the Norfolk Regiment. Anyway, of course I came. You know, we live in a strange land, don't we? I mean, there's this statue, a fig leaf over his genitals, genitals that probably rather liked the notion of another male, his friend Patroclus, perhaps. Yet people such as you and I, well, we're grotesque, aren't we?' He approached the trooper and put his hand out, touching the man's cheek very gently.

'If this is grotesque, then the world in general is ugly,' whispered the cornet player.

'Yes, I have always felt that. Too many people accept the ugliness don't they? They never fight for what is our right ... to see beauty, to perfect it, to spend time in its light. Sorry, I'm going on a bit. Look, I have a place nearby in Lowndes Square ... I have plenty of drink, and I can cook as well. Interested, my military man?'

—–—

Eddie had arranged for constables, in pairs, to patrol the length of Hyde Park, along Kensington Road and through Knightsbridge in case Eddie missed his man at his flat when he arrived, but nothing was seen of any army types walking alone or with a gentleman in civilian dress. The trooper and his new friend eluded them, and by eight they turned into Lowndes Square.

——

A few hours before, Eddie had had the flat searched, and what he saw made him rethink. It couldn't have been more ordinary. There was nothing in the sitting room or bedroom which would have been out of place in any other single man's rooms. If the constable was a monster, then this was not a lair. There was an armchair and a bamboo easy chair; in one corner there was a glass-paned bookcase and across the floor was a rich red and gold Oriental rug. Eddie knew what he was looking for though: his first search was in the escritoire, where he expected to find paper, envelopes and any other writing materials that would match the notes from 'Jack'. Then there was the murder weapon, the claw hammer – surely that would be here. His constables started their search.

'One thing is absolutely clear – and highly suspicious,' he told a constable. 'No police constable I ever knew could afford to have this kind of furniture – that escritoire is by Holland & Sons!'

'Sorry, don't follow you Guv. Means nothing to me! Though I know that my pay don't stretch to living in ruddy Knightsbridge. Whoever this peeler is, he ain't one of us.'

'Where does he get all his money?' Eddie thought aloud. 'Dockray was not robbed, or so it would seem.'

At that moment a constable in the next room shouted, 'Guv!' The officer was holding up a pair of spurs; 'Strange thing to have for a man with no 'orse.' Carney knew he had his man.

———

Eddie checked the time. 'Go to ground lads. It won't be long now if the patrols haven't already grabbed him. I want this bastard!'

They were still at the flat and the four police officers disappeared out of sight, in various back rooms. Less than fifteen minutes later, the door opened downstairs and the sound of footsteps were heard on the stairs. First into the sitting room was the cornet player. 'This is a wonderful room – you live here? A Tommy in the Norfolk Regiment?'

The other man entered and answered, 'I have other income, friend.' At this moment he was pounced on by two constables, who wrestled him to the ground and, as he yelled, Eddie sprang forward, fixing a pair of handcuffs onto the man's wrists. 'Constable Thomas Telfer, alias Jack the Jockey, you are under arrest!'

———

That night Telfer was in a cell. Standing at the door, Eddie said, 'You are not going to cheat the gallows.

You have a date with Mr Marwood. Know who he is? He's the public hangman, that's who.'

'Oh I can ride, Carney, I can ride, and I'll ride to hell with no more than a stretch o' linen!' But that night, as the Yard men watched him, Jack the Jockey wept like a child.

———

'He had been dressed as a soldier when he killed Mr Dockray, then gone out, put on his police uniform, then, of course, he was the nearest bobby when the landlady came out shouting "Murder!"' Eddie explained as the Septimus Society met for their dinner at the Oriental Hotel. 'Telfer had hidden his army gear in a garden at the corner of the street, so he was your everyday bobby after a quick change in the forsythia bush.'

'Right, let me get this right in my poor novelist's head – could be excellent material – the policeman, Telfer, went to work on another patch – A Division – then dressed as a soldier to lure his victims ... and then ... oh mercy me...' Leo Antoine always wanted clarification when a case was discussed. 'Then what about all that degeneration ... and, come to that, your other suspects – Russell and the soldier at the barracks?'

'False trails, Leo, false trails. I seem to specialise in following those!' Eddie said. 'You may use this if you like in your next sensational tale, but please change all the names, and perhaps set it in Malaysia or somewhere!' Everyone laugh. 'I freely admit I got it all wrong, what with Godfrey Russell and then the suspicions about that army orderly … might get chucked out of the Septimus I was so cack-handed with this little job, right?'

Maria lifted a glass. 'No, not at all Eddie. You were fine in the end. So, everyone, here's to the Septimus and to more successful little adventures. Shame you missed it all, George, tucked away in flat Lincolnshire.'

Glasses were raised and the toast given. 'I'm not entirely out of the picture,' said Lord George. 'My old home is in Horncastle and do you know who my neighbour is?'

There was silence. Even Professor Lacey did not know.

'Why, William Marwood, of course. He has his business there. The children all sing a little rhyme: "If Pa killed Ma, who would kill Pa? Why, Marwood!"'

The Baron's Passion

In the most untidy room at Scotland Yard, Detective Inspector Eddie Carney and his superior, Chief Constable Adolphus Williamson, were awaiting the arrival of the man who was to be selected for a very special task. Eddie, speaking energetically as usual, was gesticulating and laughing in between stories of his friend Leo.

'He's not what he seems, Dolly, and that has to be to our advantage. He puts on an act all the time. I think he's talked himself into believing that he actually is the fraud he presents to the world ... and that's why we at the Septimus love him so!'

Williamson was listening intently, his arms folded and a hangdog look on his face. He was a solid, square man, with thinning hair and a full moustache and beard, the latter being shaggy and hanging over his collar and tie. He enjoyed being unkempt and, in a way, his men liked him for it: he wasn't part of the new breed of peelers with smart outfits, peremptory orders and lists of daily objectives.

'Well the thing is, Eddie, as you are fully aware, I'm on my way out. I've been in this office for too long.

But before I go, I want to have this political business ironed out. I remember back in the sixties with them garrotters. My they were nasty beggars. But we learned how to match 'em. You knew where you were with muggers and garrotters … no real brainwork there. But this political business. Wanting to blow us up, shoot Her Majesty and God knows what else. They think they can destroy us! Imagine that!'

'Dolly, it's a grand affair now,' agreed Eddie. 'We know from reports of the ambassador and the travellers that there are people of the Devil's spawn around the streets. You're right about the old times, and the new times come on apace, right Guv? I'm as foxed as you Sir. I'm dizzy with it.'

The Chief Constable stroked his beard and looked up at the ceiling before speaking. 'Look, Eddie, back in the Crimea, when I was a new constable and full of dreams, the Tsar was reading about our strategies in *The Times*. Now, over thirty years on and I'm a greybeard loon, and nothing has changed! Why, just the other day I read a piece in some periodical all about our Easter manoeuvres, and this damned artist had followed the columns and written all about scouts watching gunboats and rattling all over East Kent with Maxim guns. I mean for God's sake, what if the conflict comes, Eddie? Well, before I hang up my hat here, I'm going to strike a blow against the enemies inside our very institution and in the bowels of the land!'

'I understand. Leo will be just the man for us. You'll think him a dolt, but beneath that naïve exterior there lurks the mind of a detective who would not be out of place in our Special Branch.'

'He's a writer, isn't he? Can't trust these writer types, son. Their minds are in the heavens and so dreamy they walk into the wall when they should be paying attention to what's coming at 'em.'

'He's fine, Sir ... he'll come good. That may be him now.' There was a knock at the door, and Leo was announced by a constable.

'Good day gents ... lovely March sunlight out there. Makes one glad to be alive, hey?'

The man the Chief Constable saw would have passed for one of the new breed of cyclists, as he wore the latest wool suit and knee breeches, canvas boots and a tweed hat. Leo had very full sideburns and a handlebar moustache that made Williamson think of a French waiter. He stood and shook hands with their visitor.

'This is Leo ... Joe actually, but to the world he is Aubrey Leo Antoine, Dolly.'

'Good Lord! You're *that* writer!' exclaimed William. 'I only yesterday finished reading your *Dangerous Journey*. What a pony express of a read, Mr Antoine.'

'Call me Leo. Everyone does, except my dear wife!'

'Do sit down and I'll have some tea brought in. Eddie, would you see to that?'

They were soon seated, and Williamson explained himself.

'Mr Antoine ... Leo ... you will no doubt be aware that there has been a great deal of talk recently about the Nihilists? There have been numerous articles in the press about bombs and Fenians. Well, that may be a little part of the picture, but there is a greater story, a sinister one, and I have asked you here to help me in destroying a nest of anarchists right here in London.'

'What? Anarchists? Tell me more, there's a book here!'

'Indeed. I'm telling you – in strictest confidence, you understand – that their activities are moving from mere propaganda to a design on the life of a prominent politician, or someone in a position of considerable power. We do not yet know who or when, but we are sure that it will happen. After all, there have been attempts to murder our dear Queen – that young madman Maclean, just eight years ago, you'll recall. He's now rotting in Broadmoor Asylum.'

'What can I do to help?' Leo asked, as a servant brought in the tea.

'Well,' said Williamson, 'I hear from Eddie here that you are a very wealthy man, and that you entertain society ... virtually all kinds of society, from actresses to earls.'

'Yes Sir. I like a party, and yes, my books, and my father's money, have made me a rich man. He was a brewer, and so I need say little more about why such profits were made here in good old England! I'll be pleased to help my country.'

'Glad to hear it. Now, out there, if you listen, you will hear the footsteps and the cab wheels and the street cries that mark the heart of our great Empire ... now imagine that to be under threat ... and from the land we have been opposed to for generations – Holy Russia! But of course this little group of troublemakers have no home – they have left Russia. They – the Brothers of Rebirth, as they call themselves – aim to remove all the old beliefs and national states.'

'Unthinkable Sir,' Leo said, sipping some tea and frowning.

'Indeed. Therefore, I am asking you to join my organisation, attached, as it were, to my Special Branch, at least in a temporary capacity. Your task will be to gather knowledge about a certain Viennese aristocrat. He is a man who loves music and the theatre, walks in the artistic circles of the city, and is generally well-liked by the higher class of Britishers. That he is from Vienna makes his deceptive public image all the more disarming. He is with no established State – he wishes to see governments and traditional power brought down low. You would be working with Madame Bellezza of course, who, as you know, is always working as our eyes and ears regarding matters European. What about it?'

Leo, whose mind was churning with the fictional possibilities of anarchists in London, leapt at the offer. 'Oh rather, yes, I am signing the contract here and now!'

Thus did Joe Sidebottom's life with Her Majesty's Secret Service begin.

———

The meeting took place at L'Église de Notre Dame de France in Leicester Place, as there had been a

meeting nearby involving some French businessmen in
Soho. Two men were in the centre of a row of pews,
one on his knees with his head bent forward in prayer.
He was young, wiry, his physique suggesting a spare
diet and much anxiety. Next to him sat an older man,
middle-aged, hunched in a thick coat, his hat on his
knees. The young man spoke first, in a Russian accent:
'Mr Maitland, I understand your problem. Your sym-
pathy with our cause is admirable and very welcome.
There is no need to worry. Our man will contact you.'

'But I do worry,' replied the older man. 'All those
publications, all the public appeals for money ...
there's plenty of feeling in favour of your country.
All I ask is that you do nothing that will lead to my
superior. He continues to write, anonymously of
course ... and you will have another payment in two
days. Goodbye, Pelriak.' He stood up and left, his
footsteps echoing through the church.

The younger man stayed and finished his prayer,
'The Lord protect my friends at home and keep them
safe from the oppression of the Okhrana and their
minions ... look after my sister ... and preserve the
spirit of Rus from tyrants.'

Behind them, out of sight but near enough to
see the smallest movement, was Maitland's superior,
a man who never missed anything that might have
a bearing on his status and security. A man with a
restless mind.

Maria de Bellezza was taking afternoon tea at home with Cara Cabrelli, the two women discussing the current dashing young men on the stage or the latest fashion for playing croquet, shopping for Fedora's new styles of boot and Spence's latest styles of travelling cloaks. Maria, however, had an ulterior motive for inviting the young actress and took out a letter from a desk drawer.

'My dear Cara, may I read you this letter from Leo? It sounds so very interesting.'

'Oh, what a novelty. Please do!' enthused Cara, her rich black hair curling down to her shoulders.

'Right, here goes,' said Maria and proceeded to read:

Dearest Maria,

I hope this letter will make your day cheery and fun! I like to think that I am a sort of ambassador for fun, of course, as I'm sure you know.

You may recall that the last time we met I mentioned a dinner to entertain my publisher and some of his friends? Well, the time is almost upon us, and I'm writing to ask if you will please play the hostess? I am, sadly, unattached, a resolved bachelor, and I am in need of not merely the feminine expertise in these matters but of your wit and charm. If you consider that to be shallow flattery, you are quite wrong.

May I also request that you could perhaps bring Cara with you too? She is a spirited young thing and would be the cause of much merriment among the males cramped into their tight dinner wear. She is so adorable. Those who fail to be charmed by your good self will unfailingly fall at her feet.

The event is at my home in Grosvenor Square a week on Friday. You know it well, of course, but I've had the whole place refurbished by Charles Melier, the famous Frenchy, since you were last here, and the place is impossibly huge.

But then, the money earned from my Dangerous books and father's business has simply run away with everything! I have twenty rooms my dear!

Now, regarding Cara. Please, please, would she sing for us? Her voice is from Heaven, dearest Maria, and here comes the real surprise: I have engaged the services of none other than Mr George Grossmith, the Savoy singer and pianist, and I even have a real Baron.

Let me know right away please. A cab will arrive for you at six if you do come. Fondest regards,

Joe

'What? He has George Grossmith coming – and did you say a *Baron?*' Cara was like a child at Christmas.

Maria matched her excitement. 'I say, my girl … you are going to sing, of course?'

Cara pretended to be coy, then struck the kind of pose an actress might for a publicity card. 'Why Madame, how could I refuse the Baron?'

———

In the Café Giraudier, in the Haymarket, Maitland and Sir David Parfitt had reached the sweet Caroline pudding and talk had moved into the desultory category. People were continually tapping Parfitt on the shoulder as they walked past, such was his popularity. He was every inch the English gentleman, knighted after his exemplary and dedicated work as military attaché in several outposts of the Empire, followed by charitable work at home with fallen women and orphaned children. It was widely known that he donated liberally to both the Broadmoor Hospital and funds to help alleviate leprosy suffering in India.

'I saw Pelriak a few days ago,' said Maitland, 'and the matter is resolved I think. Now please, allow yourself to be at ease, will you? You have plenty to smile about. Really, David, you are the man of the moment. That Foreign Secretary post is looking more likely now than this time last year.'

Parfitt nodded, but said, 'As long as there is nothing unpleasant from the wastes of Siberia – or their friends in Paris perhaps?' He was silver-haired and handsome, the hook nose and slightly narrowing chin suggesting a Roman emperor, and indeed the press had nicknamed him Marcus Aurelius, such was his reputation for serious reflection and moral rectitude. If a quotation was needed regarding the Salisbury-led Conservative Party, then Parfitt was the man. In addition, he was a prominent Christian, and prone to sermonizing.

'David, I've settled that,' said Maitland reassuringly. 'There is nothing at all to link you to these radicals. The latent boisterous student in you need have no fear.'

'I'm sure you're right, Fred, but there's a change in the air. These people have moved from printing and collecting funds to making bombs and killing Generals. What if that sort of thing crosses the Channel? Every day there is more depressing news from Russia ... why, just this morning there was a report on those students of the Agricultural Academy in Moscow being expelled. That was just for discontent. They *murdered* a Tsar, you recall, not too far back.'

'Finish your dessert and think no more of it. Pelriak is a harmless intellectual.'

At this moment an elegant lady walked past and stopped to talk to Parfitt. 'Oh I did enjoy your speech on the deceased wife's sister last week. Bravo!' she said, before moving on.

'That's Sir David Parfitt,' Maitland said with a wry smile, 'the man who says everything the upper classes want to hear ... while in his private thoughts, well, quite the opposite fills his mind ... I know you want to shake the foundations old friend.'

Parfitt, leaning closer, whispered, 'He wants to write a Nihilist novel, this Parfitt man ... seems to be popular now! To say true, this country is in need of a quake ... a quake to bring about a new way of thinking ... but we're stuck with Parliament and all that protocol and we soldier on. What would these ordinary, harmless Londoners think if they knew what I really think of all this old power? Power corrupts, of course ... so measures have to be taken.'

Parfitt held the view that the most risky topics of conversation were best done in the midst of the buzzing and hubbub of a place where people ate, laughed and shouted, such as the Café Giraudier.

No more was said and they returned to chat about the next meeting with the planning group where they would be wining and dining the great explorer, Henry Morton Stanley.

At number 34 Grosvenor Square, George Grossmith had finished his last song and stood up to take a bow and revel in the applause from the crowded drawing room. He adjusted his pince-nez and said, 'That was my new song, and I apologise for my egregious Irish accent. The title, *His Nose Was On The Mantelpiece*, bears no relation to any of Mr Sullivan's melodies so there is no need for any lawsuit to be considered.'

The gathering was amused. They loved him. Leo was acting as an amateur *conferencier*, as if the whole event was in Vienna, and he took the singer a glass of wine and invited him to stay by the piano ready for his next task. Grossmith, petite and dapper, thanked his audience once again and did a little dance step which would have been familiar to anyone who had seen him at The Savoy as John Wellington Wells, and in fact many of the present party applauded.

'Ladies and gentlemen, before we resume our conversation and allow dinner to settle – and by the way, in my home the ladies and gentlemen do not separate for post-prandial chat in their various rooms – may I ask you all to welcome two special guests. There is Baron Dieter von Merhof, all the way from Vienna, and the truly wonderful Maria de Panay Bellezza, society hostess and former wife of the late Margrave of Karnesheim.' There were cheers and clapping and both guests took a little bow. 'Now for the entertainment part of my little soirée; I would like to introduce the very talented singer and actress, Cara Cabrelli. Mr Grossmith has kindly offered to accompany her with a song from *The Pirates of Penzance* that you will surely all be familiar with, 'Poor Wandering One'.

Cara was at the far end of the room, which was cluttered with a dozen elaborate chairs and tables of ornate Rococo guilded magnificence. There were a few chaises-longue among the chairs, and a scattering of small card-tables, adorned with ormolu and mother-of-pearl. Everything was of the latest fashion, down to the huge potted plant by a solid white pillar in the middle of the right side of the room.

She arrived at the piano and Grossmith stood in order to bow, and, in return, Cara gave a curtsey. Her beautiful face and long black hair had captivated all the men, but none so much as the Baron. He had not yet had an opportunity of speaking to her, but as he strolled from talker to talker, his glance returned to Cara, as he found her irresistible. Now he moved to the front row and sat in adoration.

Cara went into Mabel's song and at each rendering of the refrain, 'Poor wandering one' the Baron sighed. When she reached the last line and sang, 'Take any heart – take mine!' he positively felt that he was twenty years old again, and not the overweight fifty-year-old he had grown into. As soon as the applause died down he was up on his feet.

Cara was surrounded by admirers, but the Baron was first to take her glove hand and kiss it. 'My little beauty, how I adore you! Ladies and gentlemen, *ein glas den damen* … let us drink to the ladies, the eternal feminine, as the great poet Goethe memorably wrote.'

Cara was speechless and blushed. The small talk carried on, and other admirers drifted away, leaving the Baron alone with her. He was a square man, sturdy and firm. Once red-haired and dashing, he was now balding and tried to compensate by growing a prominent moustache and beard. None of this, however, reduced his attraction to the fairer sex. 'My dear girl, you have entranced me. I would like you to call me Dieter. Can you do that?'

Cara smiled and nodded. As the evening wore on she found a moment to speak quietly to Maria. Seated on a leather sofa beneath a minstrels' gallery in the small sitting room, Maria said, 'My dear, Leo and I are watching the Baron. He is suspected of being possibly a little too friendly with certain Russian émigrés. You know how the city is talking about them?'

'Of course, stories have been in the papers. They are very much a threat to peaceful life, I gather.'

'Indeed. Now, how does the idea of being a tart for your country appeal?'

They laughed so much that Leo came into the room, tutting. 'Dear me, some of my guests *are* being antisocial!' It took only a wink and a flash of the eyes from Maria for him to realise that something private was being discussed and he left. Leo had a faithful following: his romances attracted the interest of the fairer sex, Lord George always said, in such a way that they would faint at the very mention of Aubrey Antoine. This was amply demonstrated now as he strode back into his broadest room, where guests had assembled to hear Grossmith play again, and offered to read an extract from his forthcoming novel, *Dangerous Embrace in the Levant*. 'With your permission, Mr Grossmith, I would like to read this before your next song.' The pianist gave a little bow and begged him to continue. The assembled party was enthralled as Leo's hero, Sir John Daring, survived a night attack by three would-be assassins. It was the perfect distraction for the Baron, who was as enraptured as anyone there.

———

In the quiet of the sitting room, hidden beneath the ridiculously overdone minstrels' gallery, Maria and Cara were whispering.

'Cara, by all means flirt with him,' Maria said. 'I know it is a challenge, but ...'

'Oh he's repulsive,' Cara retorted. 'What if he – you know, goes beyond the bounds of good manners?'

'He most certainly will. He is a dandy with a penchant for gambling and for pretty women ... but how deeply his political interests go we are not sure. We know that he has Russian friends in Vienna, and that he inherited a fortune from his banker family. Could you perhaps ... lead him on? You could torment him by saying you are married – that will really stir him up!'

When, later on, they explained the situation to Leo, he was most put out. He lamented that he was always on the margins and never actually sleuthing. Maria's response was to run her fingers through his hair, give his forehead a little kiss and say, 'My dear, Aubrey Leo Antoine is the brains of our little detective club ... in the central office, like the Scotland Yard Commissioner!'

As the ladies left him, he gave a little self-satisfied smile and murmured, 'I say, here comes the next plot ... *Dangerous Department*.'

———

Maitland dropped in to see Chief Constable Williamson at the Yard.

'Well, Dolly, I now feel rather more informed about Russian intellectuals. The one who has been troubling Mr Parfitt appears to be subject to being bought off. He's been trying blackmail, and I gave him some funds. Parfitt says he's had to have some secret meetings with this Russian. Something shady going on there, and I fear for David. But it will be the last. Next time I'll be asking you to ... remove him.'

'Sir David Parfitt himself, if I have to remind you,' said Williamson, 'is not exactly the man we read about in the papers, what with his unorthodox opinions on the vote, and on foreign policy ... and he is just one of many who wear smart coats and revel in their Oxford clubs. Who may we trust, Maitland?' The Chief Constable stared out of the window. 'You know, this world has a sickness. I'm not sure it can be cured ... not by a police force at least. The malady runs deep and has infected the bloodstream ... like a black poison, it will destroy every good thing. It will not be limited to the wilds of Russia, oh no. But perhaps I'm too old for this. I'll soon be gone from here, boring people with talk about my garden. Things are so mixed-up now. Why, a detective has to know so much, be so well-informed. The day will come when he will need a secretary following him, keeping records of all conversations. I'm tired of it all, Maitland. But I'll soon be out of your hair, and you people in the Cabinet can stop worrying about me making some awful mistake.'

'Nonsense Dolly, you're the best bloodhound we have! Now, this Baron – he has met with Pelriak. They have been seen together, but only once. There may be nothing in it. The Baron knows virtually everyone with any money in London. Their organisation is, in translation, "The Brothers of Rebirth". They want the old Russia back, and they want allies abroad. The day might come when they recruit mercenaries to go and fight the Tsar's army.'

Williamson moved across to his desk and took out a bag of sweets from a drawer, offering one to Maitland. 'I don't trust anybody. Never have. Keep following the Baron. First, he's a foreigner, and second, he speaks Russian, we know that. Those two facts make him suspicious. A peeler trusts nobody. Even my good wife is being watched – to make sure she changes the bed. I love clean sheets don't you old man?' He chuckled and Maitland joined in.

'Dolly, how many potentially dangerous Russians are in London, do you know?'

'We have these statistics coves and they pretend to know. They tell me two thousand. But that's nonsense. I always double any figure they give me. I can tell you that there are a hundred men and women who have been involved with the Paris disturbances, but they've gone to ground like damned hares. Ever hunted a hare, Maitland?'

'Can't say I have … none around Kensington, Dolly.'

'Well, you can walk up to a hare, get close, almost to the point where you think you can grab her … and then whoosh! Off she goes!'

'Hmm … so this foreign lot are like that?'

'Exactly! Now, I'm on my way to the slippers and fireside in three weeks, and they'll be giving me a trophy or a damned golden truncheon or something like that at the Grand Hotel, so the line of gossip tells me. Consequently, Maitland, I want no bomb beneath Mr Parfitt or any other prominent boy-o, right?'

'Your Mr Carney and your Special Branch are doing very well, I'm sure. My own staff are always vigilant too, you can count on that.'

'Thank you Maitland. Now you may leave me to my boiled sweets. As to the Baron, watch him like a hawk.'

When his visitor had left, Williamson sat at his desk, put his feet up on a chair and ruminated on what he had been saying about trust to Maitland. It struck him that, as he had said to himself many times before, it was more difficult to trust the men in smart suits than the stinking rough-ends of humanity that he had dealt with over the years. He pitied the poor devil who would be stepping into his shoes.

Baron Dieter von Merhof had played the rake for too long, and he knew it. He had had an epiphany, and, even in his cups, he knew it was genuine. He knew, deep in his bones, that his playing days were over, that he had been truly enchanted by the young woman, Cara Cabrelli. Even on waking up the next day with a sore head, he still smiled to himself when he thought of her. His manservant came in with eggs and toast, and the first thing the Baron said to him was, 'Kasper … I am in love!'

'Don't be foolish Sir. You have said that before, many times.'

'Yes, but this time I really am. I never believed in it but it has happened!'

'How old is the girl in question Sir?'

'Oh, twenties – early twenties.'

'Then you are in lust Sir. I know I may speak freely. You have known me for a decade.'

'Of course, tell me more.'

'There is no more to say. You are deluding yourself. When you are sober, think again, Sir.'

When Cara appeared at her next concert, a week later, the Baron was there. As she sang, he was moved to tears, and as she left the hall with her agent, he was there to give her flowers. 'My dear girl, that was wonderful … I want to ask if you would have dinner with me? Just the two of us?' She accepted.

The gifts started to arrive the next day. First there were flowers then a necklace of diamonds and a tiara. Cara reported everything to Maria and the Septimus Society monitored progress. The opinion was that if this man was involved with the Nihilists, how could he find the time to woo a woman in such a way that his days were full of romance? He appeared to have no contact with any of the leaders of the Russians in the city. Detective Inspector Eddie Carney had him followed, and his days appeared to be no more than those typically allotted to bored sons of the rich. He gambled and he drank; he dined and he sat around in clubs, but he also visited shops and bought gifts – for one woman in particular.

Their first dinner went well, until Cara told the Baron about her husband. They sat at a corner table and she was treated like a Baroness; he had all the good manners of an aristocrat, with an ability to say exactly the right words every time he answered, advised or questioned her on her life.

'I am most interested in the theatre. How did you become an actress?' he asked.

'In England, acting was never a profession for a respectable woman, Herr Baron, but times are changing.'

'You went to a school, to a college?'

Cara laughed. 'No, my dear. Thespians here simply join a company and learn as they put in the time … I have a good voice, so I soon had interesting parts, but I have also swept the dust and cleaned the doors.'

'You shall never do that again my dear!' boomed the Baron, and he was serious. Cara felt that he was genuinely revolted by her having to do such chores and judged it to be the perfect time to drop the bad news. 'No, well, now I have a husband, I have no need to work. He is quite rich.'

The Baron stopped chewing and his chin dropped. His expression was one of sheer dismay. 'My dear … this is not true! You are but a maiden, twenty-three perhaps? A girl!'

'I have a husband. He's a lawyer. I'm so sorry, Dieter, I thought we were …'

'Friends. You thought we were friends. *Ich habe eine liebesgeschichte in meinem herz …*'

'What? What are you saying Dieter?'

'I said I have a love story in my heart. And now …' He stood up, apologised, dropped several notes on the table, and left.

———

Over the following week, wherever Cara went, the Baron was there. When she appeared in a new musical play by her friend Luigi Nolliti, *The Shepherdess Queen*, he was there. The same flowers always appeared at the stage door: a bunch of lilies, accompanied by a letter of love. She was aware that, as she walked to her home in Russell Square, he was a hundred yards back, ducking away out of view when she turned.

Cara began to fret that he would soon come to realise that there was no husband. The problem was discussed by the Septimus Club, and it was decided that George was the best candidate, as he looked as a lawyer might look, and he was young enough. He and Cara went for dinner, arm-in-arm, and although neither saw the Baron, Cara felt a tingle on the back of her neck, as though they were being watched as they walked home.

At the end of the second week, Cara was at home with her maid, dressing for the last appearance in *The Shepherdess Queen*. She was busy in her boudoir and Agnes, the maid, went in and out of the sitting room, fetching and carrying a number of little things that were needed. Finally, when all preparations were virtually complete, Agnes was sent for some gloves on the side-table in the sitting room.

As the maid entered the room there was a rustling sound from across the room, somewhere behind the wide sofa. She listened intently. There it was again. Her first thought was that it was a rat or some other vermin. But then, emboldened, she spoke to the room in general: 'Whoever you are, come out from there!'

In reply, Agnes heard the words, '*Jedem das Seine* … *jedem das Seine* …' and then a crack. Peering over the sofa her eyes met those of the dying Baron. His last words were, '*Jedem das Seine* … each to his own, until Cara.'

When told the address of the shooting Eddie feared the worst, and all the way to Russell Square he expected Cara to be found dead. However, on his arrival he found the young actress weeping in her room, Agnes trying to comfort her.

Taking charge, he examined the Baron's body and searched his pockets. He found a pen, a packet of cigars, a ticket from some theatre, and a note scribbled on a piece of paper, which read:

DM thinks that he acted in a nasty and openly hostile manner last week at L's party, and he very painfully longs for forgiveness from all those who are your friends at the Grand Hotel. If DP is at the Grand on Monday 21, at 7, all will be resolved.

Eddie studied it but he could not immediately drag any sense out of it. The police work preliminaries were done, and death was confirmed as caused by a bullet to the brain. 'The maid heard the shot, and there was nobody else here. The bullet went up through the chin and into the brain. All very clear cut,' said the surgeon, leaving the cleaning up to the constables.

That evening, Eddie showed the mysterious note to Lord George and Harry Lacey at the Septimus Club.

George glanced at it and declared, 'He was mad with passion ... it's nonsense!' Eddie challenged George to a game of billiards, and they left the professor alone in the library with the note.

Harry, on the contrary, gave the text the attention he would have given a manuscript scrap of Elizabethan verse. His frown was deep and his concentration hard before he exclaimed, 'Of course! How stupid of me to take so long over it!' He ran to the billiard room, the note in his hand.

'Edward Carney, call yourself a Detective Inspector! Look, it refers to a meeting at the Grand Hotel.'

Eddie was chalking his cue. 'Well I got that, old man. But what of it?'

'Wait … there's a word formed with the first five initial letters. It's one of those announcements you have in the *Daily Graphic* or even *The Times* – you know, when families have fallen out and so on, they have these cryptic notes published. This will have been in print along with a hundred other such notes.'

'And?' Eddie asked, bored.

'Well, the word spelled out is odd … it's "Dolly".'

Eddie Carney had never moved so fast in his life. Chief Constable Williamson, he knew only too well, was to be given his retirement dinner and farewell presentation at the Grand Hotel on the Strand on Monday evening.

———

An emergency meeting was called for all those involved in monitoring the Nihilists – including members of the Septimus Society – and the note was circulated and discussed. Fred Maitland saw the importance of 'DP' immediately and snapped our orders for Dmitri Pelriak to be found and brought in.

'Then who is "DM"?' asked Maria, who had just arrived from a soirée.

'Dieter von Merhof, I would suggest ... the man who fell in love with our Cara,' Harry answered. 'He was a key member of The Brothers of Rebirth, we know that now.'

Lord George took advantage of a momentary silence. 'I say, what if it's not Pelriak? What if we arrest him and then some other DP turns up on Monday with a gun and points it at Dolly?'

'Rest assured that I'll have my men all over the Grand on Monday,' Eddie said.

———

The police and the Home Office, with all the powers and men at their disposal, could not trace Dmitri Pelriak. When Monday came, Dolly Williamson called a meeting with Maitland and Eddie. Williamson was on edge and found it hard to sit down. It was now just a matter of hours before he walked out of the building for ever, and his long career as a police officer would come to a close.

The others sat and listened while the Chief Constable gave his summary of the situation. 'Gentlemen, it now appears to be the fact, with new information, that the Baron was, shall we say, the trading depot between killers in the service of anarchist mayhem and those backroom sorts who never show their faces in public and who plot the most nefarious deeds, such as sending me to the next world. In addition, gentlemen, it seems that our rat has scuttled out of sight into his sewer.

This Russian intellectual is nowhere to be found. In my experience, there is one reason for this: he is disguised. Yes, Mr Pelriak is most likely now walking around the East End with the appearance of a very hairy Jewish gentleman, or he could be a coster among a hundred costers screaming out the price of apples. You see my line of thought?'

They nodded.

'Therefore, the question arises: what should be done?'

Eddie looked up to see Williamson doing some very energetic beard-stroking. 'Well, he's going to be at the Grand at seven, and we'll have an army waiting for him Guv!'

'Or we hold my retirement somewhere else entirely, and still have an army at the Grand. Of course, such has been the vigour of our search that the chances are he knows we're after him and he's left for Siberia,' Williamson muttered. 'I shall inform my staff to switch to the Hotel Metropole on Northumberland Avenue … they do the finest mutton cutlets in London. Eddie, in the event that our man is of low brain capacity and still insists on turning up with a pistol at the Grand, we'll have him. Maitland, would you issue a sketch of Pelriak across the stations and to all of Eddie's men? The Grand is huge. He must know that the event would be in the great central dining hall – broad enough to house a regiment for a meal! You'll have to take the whole of E Division to surround the hall.'

'Me?' said Eddie, surprised. 'I'm to miss your last dinner, Guv?'

'Last dinner? You seem to think I am bound to leave this vale of tears permanently!'

'Dolly, there is one point,' said Maitland. 'Does Pelriak know what you look like? Would he have seen a picture of you?'

'Excellent question, Maitland. To my knowledge there has been no newspaper picture of me for the last five years. I never talk to those scribblers from Fleet Street. They write nothing but dirt.'

'Then in that case, there *will* be a man receiving a retirement gift and presentation tonight at the Grand – myself!' declared Eddie, rapping the table with a sense of triumph. 'We'll trap the rat.'

—·—

Everything was in place at both hotels that night. At the Metropole, Williamson gathered with dozens of his old partners, sergeants, office workers and retired constables. The dinner was prepared for sixty guests, and at nine thirty, awash with his favourite red wine, Adolphus spoke, mixing reminiscences with some pleasantries, becoming increasingly the man they knew as 'Dolly' rather than the Chief Constable.

'We live in changing times … and I leave the force in the good hands of Commissioner Monro … James … stand up and take a bow. My friends, there are all kinds of new ideas and new people at the Yard, but I have to speak as a beat bobby, a war-horse of these London streets, and I know that policing is, at heart, about working to fashion good relations with the public,' he paused for the applause and shouts of agreement.

———

In the massive dining hall of the magnificent Grand Hotel on Trafalgar Square, tables had been set up beneath the massive ornate pillars reaching to the glass ceiling, and the attendants sitting at the tables, pretending to dine, were all armed police. As they chattered their colleagues were in the shadows, firearms at the ready. If the assassin was coming, they would be ready.

———

'Changing times, yes, but exciting times too,' said the Chief Constable, now in full flow. 'I have this sensation of leaving at exactly the time when matters are hurtling towards a distinctly international arena. My old friends, be ready to take on threats from across the oceans, that's what I feel in my bones … and I know you all always trusted that very unscientific aspect of my sleuthing … but I thank you all for coming, and for giving me this wonderful and very heavy golden cup, with such a thoughtful inscription: "To the Chief, Adolphus Williamson" – only my wife calls me that, and that's when I'm in trouble!' Dolly paused to allow some laughter at that. The audience at the Metropole was having a memorable time.

———

The Grand Hotel had a huge, sweeping staircase, but clearly that was not the route that Pelriak would take. Eddie had surveyed the place, and found two other pathways through the building which would lead to the dining hall. 'He will almost certainly come this way ... through the service area where the trolleys come out,' Eddie instructed his three sergeants, as they made ready for their visitor.

———

It was Harry Lacey who had the revelation. He was reading the latest edition of *Punch* at the Septimus Club and was feeling quite relaxed, in spite of his Rossiter restraint corset, with its steel band and whalebone supports. The little half-column he had alighted on was headed, 'Parfitt's Political Refusals' and it was an account of his fondness for Socialist philosophy in his youth, and his love of church ritual. One phrase struck him: 'The possible next Foreign Secretary, we learn, is a quiet Russophile, and last night he told the assembled students at the Guildhall that our political structures must change or die.'

It was at first a mere inkling, a foreboding, like the shadow of a cloud across a lawn on a sunny day. But then it clarified, and he sprang up, launching the magazine into space, and cried out, 'Sir David Parfitt!'

The aged Earl of Clannmore grumbled in disapproval at having his snooze disturbed at this outburst, but Harry was already out of the club like a grey-hound and calling for a cab.

———

In the Metropole Williamson's speech was complete and the guests were gradually dispersing, with firm handshakes and promises to stay in touch. The Chief was now left with just one old friend, James Munro. He was growing a little weary of the man's anecdotes, but remained patient, as they had been new bobbies on the beat together, decades ago.

'Yes, James, we had a lot to learn then, old man. You've come a long way, and, of course, it's your turn next to stand up here and give a farewell speech!'

No one recognised Sir David Parfitt as he entered the Metropole, as he was wrapped in a grey double-breasted wool frockcoat, the collar up and covering the lower half of his face. He walked through the throng of police officers, on their way to catch trains, cabs, or simply walk home through the city streets. There was heavy rain outside now, and all were swathed in coats and hats, scarves and gloves. No one noticed the man in the grey frockcoat, tightly clutching a knife in one of the deep pockets.

Dolly was strolling out of the dining room, still chatting with his sergeant, when the man approached and shouted, 'Chief Williamson!' Then, as the knife blade glinted in the air, another voice cried out, 'Sir David ... it's you!'

Parfitt turned and came face-to-face with Harry Lacey. 'It's you ... I know it's you ... say farewell to life!' He swung around and plunged the knife into Harry's midriff before the professor could pull out the pistol he always carried in his inside pocket. Harry clutched his stomach, before slumping to the marble floor.

As Parfitt spun back towards the Chief Constable, Williamson struck him on the temple with his newly acquired golden presentation cup.

As Parfitt fell to the floor, unconscious, Harry struggled to his feet.

'By God, man ... you're all right!' exclaimed Dolly.

'Yes ... I have the Rossiter Manform Retainer to thank for that ... the damned blade struck the steel band!'

The policemen had no idea what the professor was talking about.

'I expect Dmitri Pelriak is on the way to some bug-infested den out towards Essex, feeling like a hunted fox, but here's the DP who was their killer.'

'Whose killer?' asked Dolly, perplexed. 'This is Sir David Parfitt.'

'I think you'll find he led a double life, Sir. He was a link in the chain of The Brothers of Rebirth.'

'Well I'm amazed that they would want to top me, a man of no importance now!' Dolly managed to chuckle at his own words.

'Ah, it was a gesture ... an ignoble gesture, Sir!' said Harry, before leaving to find Eddie and share a well-earned drink with the Detective Inspector.

The Honourable Man

London, the great hub of the Empire, was at its zenith in 1890, and the men who oiled the wheels of the great machine that was Britain earned their respect through hard work, dedicated study and focused concentration on how they might rise. To rise in society was the aim: to rise through merit was arguably a much rarer phenomenon than stepping up the hierarchy by questionable means. Yet there was nothing questionable about Sir John Tardow. At the opening of that momentous decade, the Forth Bridge may have been a new wonder of the world, but it was not the only topic of conversation at dinner and concert intervals. For the first six months of the year the name on everyone's lips was Tardow. The future of the country was safe in the hands of men such as he, said *The Times*, so it was to be a valued estimation.

Tardow was the son of an elementary school teacher, and by the age of thirty he had a business of his own. He had seen the potential of waste products in an Industrial Revolution and he had found uses for trash, refuse and any number of throwaway substances and created markets for them.

However, his reputation did not end with the effluents of society. He also created great, national commercial organisations and lobbied Parliament for the promotion of radical schemes to alter the face of the land. Then, in 1881, when still a young man of only forty-three, he invested in railways, and soon found himself to be one of the richest men in the land. It seemed that the man who was born in the year of Victoria's coronation was destined to epitomize the age of prosperity, an era which produced The Great Exhibition and subdued the Indian Mutiny; constructed a steel industry and built locomotive tracks across continents.

In the autumn of 1891 Tardow was on the verge of joining Parliament, as a Gladstonian Liberal, with the elections looming the following year.

And he was happy, until, one cold morning in January 1890, when his servant brought the post to the breakfast table. His wife, Floriana, was still in bed, suffering with a headache. He opened the first letter – a handwritten note – and read:

Rich Man Sir,

Time the world of London knew about Flo don't you think?
Who she was, and her former (oldest) profession. She knows me.
Ask her about Theo Sachs. Ready money would keep your secret.
Flo knows where I am.

Tardow was a man who prided himself on his self-control and discipline; he let memories of Paris seduce him away from his mounting anger. He saw her face, heard her laugh, felt her kiss as if it were happening again. His Floriana, named after the German composer, Robert Schumann's imaginary character, Florestan. It had been a courtship of dances, parties, and long evenings when too much drink was taken but in which poems, songs and laughter filled the air. He had been twenty-two then, and love had found a place in his life for the first time.

She had arrived in his life with a chuckle of amusement, as he sat alone in a café, scribbling in his diary. She had asked what he was writing. He had been affronted at this breach of good manners, but then remembered he was in Paris, and asked her to sit with him. He ordered coffee. By that evening they were holding hands and he was on the verge of making promises.

The dream dissolved as she came into the room and said good morning. He rose to kiss her cheek and asked if she was feeling better. Inside, a thousand questions were bubbling up.

'Oh *ma chere*, when I see you I am well!' She helped herself to eggs and mushrooms from the sideboard, and sat down opposite him. Her grey eyes and auburn hair had brought spring, he thought, into January. The servant brought her tea.

'Flora, my love, may I ask you a question? Do you know a man called Theo Sachs?'

He could see by her face that she did. She dropped the fork she had just picked up with a clatter onto her plate. Tardow picked up the letter and passed it across to her.

'I've ... I've given him money, John! He knows all about me.' He could see tears welling up in her eyes and she dabbed at them with her handkerchief. 'I should have told you ... but ... but ...'

'You thought he would go away.'

'I gave him fifty pounds, and then another fifty pounds. He promised he would leave me alone after that. I hate him!' She spoke the last words with venom and slammed her hand down on the edge of the table.

John tried to comfort her, reassuring her that everything would be all right. But they both knew that the past had blown into their contented lives like a chill wind on a summer's day. When finally they sat down to talk, away from the servants, Flora, kneeling on the carpet at the side of Tardow's armchair, held his hands and looked up into his face with teary eyes.

'John, the Floriana Daria you met all those years ago ... I was always honest with you ... I told you all about my life, yes? You know my other name ... my professional name?'

'Of course my dear. I feel confident that I know all about you. We neither of us has secrets.'

'This man, Sachs, he will say the most terrible things about me. He will tell the press that I am ... was ... a harlot.'

'My love, he will never be believed,' soothed Tardow.

His wife suppressed a sob. 'John, the papers will call me a *courtesan*. Everyone will know that I have a past ... a past that any woman would feel ashamed of.'

'We'll talk no more of this today. I shall walk to the office, as usual. You must meet your friends for the lunch you planned. I promise you that I will end this!'

They tried, with a supreme effort, to pretend that there was no problem, that nothing was capable of shaking the balance and order of their world together. But two days later a second letter came.

Mr Tardow,

Further to my letter the other day, you know that your dear wife knows where to find me, and I expect £200 to be delivered to that address within the next 48 hours. Should this not happen, I will be pleased to tell the newspapers all about little Meg Caley of Spitalfields, and how she was so skilled in entertaining Gentlemen.

More than a mere threat hangs over you. I have made a statutory declaration with a magistrate. Therefore any rash action from you will lead to a confirmation of your infamy and indeed of your living a life of deceit and hypocrisy. Mr Theo Sachs, solicitor.

Tardow decided to pay the man a call, soon finding his address now that he knew he was a solicitor. The office was what he expected: a dingy, neglected box of a place a few streets behind Covent Garden.

When Sachs saw the loping gait of a tall man dressed with the same elegance as a lord of the realm, he sensed that the man he expected was here at last. Tardow did not even knock at the door. He strode in, eyes fixed on Sachs, who was sitting behind a desk heaped with paper. Tardow's imposing figure cast a shadow over the desk, and the short, round-bellied man sitting behind it flicked back a coif of oily hair and instinctively straightened up.

'How good of you to come Mr Tardow.'

'I ought to throttle you here and now, you snake!'

'Albert!' Sachs called out, inclining his head back towards what appeared to be no more than a cupboard. Behind him a door creaked open and a child of perhaps thirteen peeped out. 'Yes Mr Sachs?'

'You are able to hear everything we say in here?'

'Course Mr Sachs. I ain't deaf!'

'Good, now carry on with that copying.'

Tardow slammed his cane against the man's desk, making him start.

'Easily frightened, Mr Sachs? Well, that is not the case with me. I have brought no money, and references in your note to a statutory declaration mean not a jot to me. I suggest you crawl back into the noxious hole you crawled out of and forget your dreams of milking me or my wife for any more money. It will not happen!'

Sachs leaned back and licked his lips. 'Delicious woman, that girl. I knew her once; what was she called, now what was it … oh yes, Meg Caley … lived in Spitalfields, daughter of a poor weaver on hard times. She was, shall we say, *extending favours*, to save dear Pa from the workhouse. I did appreciate those favours, Mr Tardow.' He gave a soft sigh and pursed his lips. In a second, Tardow's cane had swung out and rapped him sharply across the face. There was a scream of pain and Sachs fell from his chair, clutching his cheek. From the door Albert was craning his neck to look into the office. 'You saw that assault?' Sachs screeched at the boy. 'You saw him strike me?'

'Goodbye Mr Sachs. You will not hear from me again. But should you approach me – or my wife – one more time, you can expect more of the same.'

Tardow felt sure that fear would rid him of the nuisance. But he was wrong.

———

'Here it is in the bleedin' paper,' he said to himself, taking another swig from the whisky bottle. 'This is my man.' He put the page of newsprint to his lips and kissed it. Then he staggered to his feet, checked his face in the cracked mirror by the sink and laughed. 'Private Garvey, Sir, reporting for duty,' he said with a salute. Looking back at him was a shaggy mop of black hair flecked with grey, a ruddy face, swollen eyes and a stubbled chin.

He took a few steps, grabbed a bayonet case from the sideboard, and sat down again, drawing the blade out and running his finger over it. 'Jack Garvey, still removing scum from this piss-pot of a world. It ain't no Christian place like my Pa said ... no, no, no. It's a fallen world ... fallen. There's devils out there needin' to bleedin' die.'

He let his head sag backwards onto the back of the armchair and let a memory in. He was ahead of his escort. It was 1882 and they were in a Kashmir valley in Gilgit. Accompanied by some Ghurkas and

Pathans, he ordered all but his guide, the Khazi from Dir, to walk ahead and survey the next bend in the valley. He was about to speak when he heard movement behind, turned, and saw the Khazi throwing his breech-loader away, about to take his sword. He did this in seconds and ran at Jack, ready to thrust the blade into him. He floored the man with his fist, and as the Khazi tried to run off, he tackled him and held him down flat. Then his Ghurkas came to help. It was a close-run thing.

Coming round again, he thought of the next assignment. 'Ah Sergeant Bayonet, you will earn the corn, settle the Lord's dues,' and he allowed the deep guttural rattle of a drunken laugh to engulf him.

———

Lord George and Harry Lacey were playing chess in the library of the Septimus Club. Strangely for Harry, he was insisting on chatting during the supposed silence when concentration was required before the next move was confirmed. George usually won, but Harry had been improving lately. 'I think I ought to talk on strychnine on Friday, George. Excellent subject … a number of cases I could refer to. Course my doctor has told me to play more cricket, and the match with the Writers' Eleven should be just the thing.'

'Do stop prattling Harry, I'm feeling combative and wish to thrash you. Anyway, what you talk about at the Oriental dinner is immaterial. The Septimus brains will be distinctly dulled by the time you stand up and play the Professor.'

'You may be right. But the cricket match … I understand that Conan Doyle and his friend Alf Mason will both play … dashed good batsman, Mason.'

There was a shout of triumph. 'Checkmate! Got you again, Prof!' George beamed and took a cigarette from his case, but he did not light it, as at that moment Smythe brought in a red-faced visitor. 'Mr John Tardow, My Lord.'

Greetings were exchanged and soon Mr Tardow was telling his story to two attentive listeners.

'This requires the utmost discretion, My Lord, and er … Professor Lacey.' They nodded. 'As you may know, my wife is … well, you have no doubt read the papers this last week.'

'Yes, but we treat them as purveyors of fantasy, Mr Tardow,' said Harry.

'Right … well, you seem to be aware of my situation. What you will not know gentlemen is how deeply I love my wife, and how, although the allegation that we lived together out of wedlock for a few years is true, and indeed although her early life was a rack of torment applied by poverty, we love each other very much. When I met her I was a young man with ambitions and little knowledge of the fairer sex, you understand. As time wore on, she became the most precious thing in my life. When this vermin appeared and threatened to take everything from us, I acted rashly.'

'Rashly? Please explain,' said George, interested.

'I went to his office and, well, I struck him.'

'Oh dear,' said Harry.

'But that is not the worst of it. I have, I fear, done something extremely foolish.'

'Oh dear God, what have you done?' asked George.

'I have hired a killer,' Tardow whispered, with a shifty look around the room. But there were only two other men in the library: the Earl of Clannmore was deeply asleep and the Earl of Backforley was deranged and dreaming of his days in Basutoland.

'*What?* By the shooting stars of heaven, you surely have not?' hissed George. Harry, who had been sipping his brandy, spluttered out 'Blood and sand!'

'I understood, from my friend Maria de Bellezza, that you gentlemen could be relied on to help anyone with legal difficulties ... and that you could be relied upon for discretion, and of course, for professional scruples ...'

'Stop!' cried George. 'You have already implicated us in this murderous plan?'

'Well, that's the dilemma. I did not conceive of the folly of this until I realised that I was dealing with a man who is himself capable of taking life. I have only learned since talking with him at the Frying Pan and ...'

'Stop again!' said George firmly. 'Did you say you met him at the Frying Pan public house ... in Brick Lane?'

'Yes.'

George and Harry looked at each other in sheer stupefaction.

'The man was an old soldier, I believe. My servant knew someone at the place and set up a meeting, knowing that I needed what I believe is called a mugger and a rampsman.'

'Those terms are not applied to killers, Mr Tardow. It appears you met a robber.' George frowned.

'Look, I went along to that tavern and asked for him. Captain Clinker he was called, a military man. He was there, and he was somewhat light-headed with drink. I asked him to help me and he named a price ... I never mentioned murder. I asked for the man in question to be *frightened*. That was the word I used ... but when I told my servant that I'd met Captain Clinker he told me that the man was not the one he had in mind, and he had no notion whatsoever with whom I had been speaking. He said he'd arranged for me to meet someone called Langer, but when Langer wasn't there, the landlord brought Clinker to me. I thought he was the same kind of cove!'

'Then why do you think this Clinker will try to kill Sachs?' George asked.

'Well, the soldier left, and then I went to leave as well but the landlord took me to one side and said, *"You'll be fine there ... he'll blow the man out of this world, Guv."* Then he winked at me.'

'Mr Tardow, Clinker is a false name, of course,' George said. 'But you must not be anxious ... you will never hear from this man again.'

'Oh, that's a pity ... I gave him money!'

'*What?* This gets worse,' Harry said, 'Let us establish the facts now. You went to this public house, hired some robber to instill fear into a man ... but you do not know the robber's real name nor his address. Then you come along here to ask ... what exactly?'

Tardow looked sheepish. 'Well, I paid him twenty pounds and promised another twenty if Sachs was ... well, subdued.'

George and Harry moved across to the long bookcase that ran behind their favourite sofa and whispering was heard. On their return they requested John Tardow to listen carefully. Harry adopted the stance he used when about to give a lecture on Petrarchan sonnets, put his hands under his coat-tails, then smoothed his moustache.

'Now, Mr Tardow, as our friend Maria will have told you, the Septimus Club helps various people in matters impinging on criminal behaviour. We tend to concentrate, for the most part, on cases for which the police force have little time or for which they need our particular expertise. Now, what we generally do *not* do is aid and abet people who have themselves transgressed ... however, in this instance, it seems that you are asking us simply to trace a former soldier – one of a possibly violent disposition – and attempt to stop him taking the life of a solicitor. Does that all meet with your approval?'

'Yes, for God's sake, stop him. I am suing Sachs for libel. I have set that in motion. In my stupidity I suppose that I thought that if I could scare him off, there

would be no need for the libel prosecution to progress
… my wife would have to give evidence, of course,
and I only came to see after setting matters in motion
that perhaps she would find it all intolerable!'

'Very well then. The Septimus Club will begin the
search for Captain Clinker before anything tragic
happens. In the meantime, you are on course for the
law courts, and surely that will be the only proper way
to beat this guttersnipe?' Tardow nodded. 'I've been
very irrational … not at all like me. Thank you gentlemen. Please, keep me informed.'

'One moment, Mr Tardow,' said Harry, taking out
his notebook and pen. 'We'll need a description of
this Clinker.'

'Well, it was quite dark … but he had a round,
bloated face, with long dark hair and … no beard,
but not well shaven either. I thought him a fighting
man, as he had that broken nose that pugilists tend
to have. I would say with some conviction that he
was not yet forty years of age – perhaps mid-thirties.
He was singing something … something like, *All he did
was kiss me but my heart began to fly.*'

'That's very useful,' Harry said and proceeded to
sing a line from the song. '*My heart began to fly, and I'm
so happy I could cry* … Molly McCardle sings it … she's
down at the supper club as a rule.'

'Ah, one more thing,' said Tardow. 'He was a
Yorkshireman. I've dealt with a number of men from
that shire in my business. He had that very distinctive speech … *tha knaws.*' The last two words were so

incongruous that they all managed a smile. 'He also had a medal of some kind, pinned on his coat.'

'A medal? What shape was it? What design?' Harry pressed.

'It was dark! I would say it had leaves … maybe a flower of some kind? It had four leaves, I think. And there was a badge sewn on his coat. That was a flower also, and there were two words over the flower.'

George seized on this detail. 'This is vitally important. What was the motto?'

'It was in Latin. I never studied the language, My Lord. Unlike you varsity men, I attended a modern school. The curriculum was commercial. French was the other language.'

'Well, think … think about the words,' Harry urged.

'Oh … something vegetable. I thought of a vegetable … can't think what it was.'

'Mr Tardow, if you think of anything else, let us know, and if you remember the motto, tell us immediately,' said Harry.

'In the meantime, my libel suit goes on … I dread seeing Flora in that witness box, tortured by Sachs … for he will defend himself of course! Now I must leave you, and I hope there is something which may be done gentlemen!' Tardow said his goodbyes and left.

When their visitor had gone, George turned to Harry, who was nibbling an iced bun. 'That was strange in the extreme. We were discussing a possible murder and yet we found some humour … he is a remarkable man … and what the deuce was the medal?'

'Yes … and a vegetable! What regiment has a vegetable on its escutcheon?' asked Harry.

'Let us summarize the situation, Harry.' George paced the room, annoying the titled old men trying to snooze. 'Here is a wealthy man with a high reputation in the world of business, and a wife with a less than respectable past. Then along comes a snake in the grass who blackmails first the lady and then our John Tardow. The good husband does what we all would do: he confronts the man, but realises that the law, not the fist, would better accomplish a settlement. But then …'

'Then he sees that an action for libel has to be done, but that an ordeal in court would ruin them anyway!' interrupted Harry.

'Yes, old man … hence the desperate employment of a killer.' Lord George looked pensive and then asked, 'What facts to we have, Harry?'

'Our assassin is not young – probably thirty-something years old. He has a broken nose. He has a regimental medal … with a motto suggesting a vegetable. There is also another flower-like badge sewn on his coat.'

'We have to find this man before he finds Sachs,' said Lord George.

'Indeed,' answered Harry, 'but we have to find Sachs first.'

Jack Garvey was sitting in an alley by an old fruit box, re-reading the article in the *Daily Telegraph*:

Mrs Tardow's Alleged Immoral Past

There was considerable moral outrage expressed yesterday at our offices when it was revealed to us by Mr Theo Sachs, a London solicitor, that Mrs John Tardow, thought to be of French birth and education, was in fact, so he alleges, a woman engaging in street prostitution while living in Spitalfields in the early 1860s. Mr Sachs has informed us that he is to be prosecuted for libel by her husband, the man of business recently engaged in politics, and thought to be a strong candidate for representing Forley Water at the forthcoming elections.

He read no further. Concentrating on the print tired his eyes. 'Well, Mr Sachs, I got your address, I got your name in here ...' he grunted and tapped a finger to his temple. He struggled to his feet, stood to attention, arms by his side. The world he knew dissolved into a blur and he was in barracks again.

'Then there's the money, Jack. You need to 'ave the money, old soldier. Without that it's ruin, old matey, ruin.' He rifled his pockets for the notes, and out came a wad of dirty old notes, and, from another pocket, a handful of silver coins, all spread out on his little box. 'Ha ... safety. That's what you got if you 'ave these, Jack ... safety. A bed for a night is four pence ... you got a lot of beds here.'

Sergeant, Sir, ready for inspection, Sir. Yes there is the trunk o' mine with everything laid out proper like. I got the soles of my boots up-turned, and see the gloves, white as snow, Sergeant. There's my hat, my cuffs, my straps ... all ready Sir! He gave a wobbly salute. Then he staggered forward, lurching towards the filthy pavement. Laughing to himself, he sat back down on the pavement and took out a bottle of rum from the pocket in his greatcoat. 'Yes, Mr Sachs, I got your name and I'm coming to pay you a visit. The scum has to go. Yes, the little louse has to go. The enemy Sir, the heathens … they have to go!'

That's my kit Sir. Everything in its place as required. Yes, I brushed everything, I scrubbed everything. I been on me knees for the regiment, Sir. Die for the regiment, I would, Sir. Attention! Go forward soldier. May I stay with this officer, Sir? He's been hit. He's down and he needs attention, Sir. I'm used to dealing with blood Captain. He's bleeding badly and I could stay with him Sir, until he dies Sir, for his country. Permission granted. Thank you Sir, from the bottom of me 'eart.

———

Sachs was almost buried under a heap of papers when the door opened and a smart, well-built man walked in. 'Mr Sachs? I'm Detective Sergeant Davis, of the Yard.'

'Oh right. What can I do for you?'

'Well I'm here to help you Sir … in relation to a Mr Tardow.'

Sachs's face screwed up. 'Ah, so you know about the libel case? But I see no reason why I should be interviewed. I've done nothing.'

Davis sat down without permission. 'Personally, I think what you've done is despicable, but I'm a peeler and supposed to have no opinion, Sir.'

'What *I've* done? Have you seen what he did to me?' Sachs pointed to the angry red wheal across his cheek.

'Indeed Sir. Are you familiar with the word blackmail?'

There was a pause. 'You are here to charge me then?' asked Sachs.

'Not at all Sir. I'm here to protect you. Seems that somebody ... can't say who ... might want to do you harm.'

'You mean Tardow of course?'

'Let's just say *someone*.'

'I see, and so someone at the Yard thought that I might be a target? I wonder who could bear such emotions towards me? I have no enemies in the world detective.'

'Well, in case you have, I got my little friend here,' Davis tapped his chest, 'a Mauser pistol. Got any tea?'

———

'Eddie, I've come for some help.' Harry sat in his friend's office in Scotland Yard, trying his best not to upset the detective, who looked decidedly downhearted.

'Can you give us some constables to walk around some beer shops and such?'

'What on earth for, Harry?' He rubbed his head. 'Oh dear – I drank some beer last night ... I'm sure it was off. My head has native drums in it. Now what's the play?'

Harry put on his lecturing voice. 'Right. Basic facts of the case. We need to find a soldier, in his thirties, maybe forty, Yorkshire, has long hair, goes to public houses around Brick Lane. He may frequent several, but should be known at the Frying Pan. He has a broken nose. Smythe has been to the public house and had no luck. Nobody knows the man.'

'In a half-mile of that place I guess we have thirty beer shops and pubs, Harry! How many constables do you want? Have you nothing else?'

'Well, I'm working it out … now, let's say this man left the army recently, around five years ago. I've asked the War Office (or rather George has, as he was at Eton with four gentlemen who are now brigadiers) to provide muster rolls and discharge records … but we need the regiment! Apparently this man had medals … and some motto to do with vegetables. Make sense?'

'Now Harry, you're talking more nonsense than usual. But we do have a list of regiments, with mottos.' Eddie shouted for someone and as a constable came to the door, he requested the list. 'You wouldn't believe just how many former military men we have causing trouble, and the prisons are packed with them, of course. It's understandable when you think what war does to a man. They are discharged from army life and either live on a pittance or thin air, and of course they are very skilled at drinking away anything rattling in their pockets!'

A folder arrived and Eddie pulled out a bunch of sheets and handed them to Harry. 'Here we are. You start on those and I'll check these here.'

They read in silence, then Eddie muttered, 'No, no cabbages or peas…' Then Harry exclaimed, 'By God … surely this is it … *Celer et Audax.*'

'Don't follow you Harry.'

'*Celer et Audax* … Swift and Bold. It's the motto of the King's Royal Rifles Corps. We can get the man's name now, surely!'

Eddie looked baffled, then Harry passed the sheet across and the Detective Inspector saw it at once. 'Ah! Celery! Well done Prof.'

'I need to know which men have been discharged within the last five years or so … where they fought last,' said Harry. 'I have to go, Eddie … what about the searches?'

'Right. Tonight – all drinking holes in a half mile radius of the Frying Pan. If we must act, it best be quickly! But you know what you need – a drawing of the man.'

'A drawing? Mr Tardow could possibly supply some details, but the difficulty lies in the fact that he met this soldier in semi-darkness.'

'Ah, then it may not be possible. You will be able to find a list of men discharged within a set period, but that may still leave hundreds.' Eddie racked his brains, trying to think of another approach. 'Though of course, you have a rough idea of his age … that should help.'

'Yes, and almost certainly born in Yorkshire.'

It was food for thought, but Harry had no time to spare. He was heading for the War Office.

——

There was a search of pubs and beer shops and as Jack Garvey walked along he could not fail to notice that there was something of moment going on. He asked a man lounging by the corner of Newgate Street what was the commotion.

'Peelers after some poor beggar. I heard they was after a soldier, so my mate says.'

That was more than enough for Jack. In seconds he was heading towards the one friend he had if he needed to disappear. Ernie Smith, a photographer now but once a Tommy, had his studio over the City Toy Shop on west Cheapside.

He scuttled past the statue of Sir Robert Peel, and at that point he felt dizzy. He stumbled into a bollard and one knee slammed into the metal, a stab of pain shooting up his leg. *You're falling apart, Jack, get 'old of yourself!* he muttered, before diving around the corner behind the toyshop to the back entrance. Climbing the stairs, he knocked on the door, shouting out for Ernie.

Ernie, a dapper little man with a pipe stuck in his mouth, half opened the door and squinted through the space. 'Now my old mate,' he said, 'long time no see. What's the trouble? I can see you got some.'

'Well, if you let me in I'll …'

'Can't do that old matey, got people in.'

'What? People … Ernie, it's me, Jack. The man what stood beside you at Kaffie Dowar. Let me in … there's peelers after me.'

There were calls from behind the door. Jack could hear people laughing.

'This is my business, Jack, my occupation now. That soldiering, it was a long time back … anyway, what have you done?'

'I done nothing. Well, petty theft … I think they want me for a little fight what I had when a cove didn't want to give me his pocketbook.'

There were more calls from behind, and Ernie, again full of apologetic sounds, closed the door.

Rage rose in Jack's breast and he slammed his fists against the door, shouting Ernie's name. From somewhere below a voice thundered out, 'Shut up will ya!'

It was too much. His knee throbbed with pain; his head was sore, and he felt a shiver of fever rush through him. He felt his legs give way and he slithered down the door. He felt in his pocket for the whisky bottle and desperately raised it to his dry lips.

Right then … pull yourself together, soldier. Covent Garden. You got an order, Tommy. You need to see Mr Sachs and give him some blade, let him meet mister death, like what them Gyptians got. But not yet … you need some golden water, boy, some drink of the bleedin' Gods. He began to laugh, uncontrollably, louder and louder, so that more voices shouted for him to shut up.

Bedford Street, Jack, number fourteen … Bedford Street, number fourteen … Mr bleedin' Sachs. He made a determined effort to struggle to his feet and gauge exactly where he was, in which direction he had to walk. Out on the street again, he saw the blur of passers-by and called out to no one in particular, 'Covent Garden ... which way mate?'

Someone pointed and said, 'Keep going, up here.'

Whisky back in his pocket and his bayonet tucked in his broad leather belt, Jack Garvey forced himself along the pavement, eyes straight ahead, arms swinging. *Quick march, you lads, I want a straight line ... straight line!* The words of the long-time dead played again in his mind: *Permission to stay with this officer Sir? He's got blood seeping out of him Sir, and we have to do the right thing by this young man, Captain. Thank you Sir. I'll attend to the young man Sir ... I'll sit with him ... ducking bullets? Yes, I'll not mind the bullets Captain. Pray to the God of war p'raps, Sir, like us all did in India ... same 'ere Sir, among the Gyptians, Sir. I'll stay with him.*

———

Lord George's contacts and influence had paid off, Harry thought, as he sat by a desk in the innards of the War Office at Whitehall, waiting for a clerk to bring someone to help with his search. It was a daunting place, and everyone's manner had been hard and peremptory as he arrived and announced himself, but at the third interview, at last a face had responded with a smile and said, 'Ah yes, Lord Lenham-Cawde told me about the problem.'

The clerk arrived, but not accompanied by papers or boxes of files. He had a smart little man in a dark suit by his side. 'Professor Lacey? I'm Colonel Ranger, Intelligence.'

They shook ands and walked across to the foyer where there were tables and chairs. Someone brought tea, and they sat. 'Professor, George tells me that you are … how shall I say … sleuths? George always liked the murder stories in the worst kind of penny dreadful rubbish!'

'We might be amateur, but by God, if we don't shift tonight, a man may die.'

'Right … well, in Intelligence we gather facts; we keep records, produce gazetteers, that kind of thing. Now, I had my man look at the muster rolls and the discharges for the regiment. Using a little commonsense and inference, I would say your man was in Egypt back in '82. This was the Arabi business … your man would have been around twenty-five, let's say. There was some rather testing scrapping going on. He's a tough man, your Yorkie broken nose … let's call him that for now.'

The colonel had been holding a few sheets of paper that the clerk had given him. 'Now, your man said he had a medal that looked like a flower … well, the King's Royal Rifle Corps' badge looks like a four-leaved flower – your Mr Tardow would have seen that.'

Harry was increasingly impressed with the measured tone and delivery in which the colonel spoke. Another sheet of paper was put on the table. 'Now,

I sat down and compiled a list of men of around thirty-five who were born in God's own county … as my father used to call it, as he was born in Leeds. Now, there is this matter of the other medal.' He frowned and rubbed his chin, thoughtfully. 'Now if you will allow me to play detective for a second, Professor, could I clarify that this other medal had two words over it?'

'Yes, that's what Tardow said,' Harry replied.

'Now, in Egypt at that time, some of the regiment were operating as mounted infantry …'

'*Mounted* infantry, Colonel Ranger?' interrupted Harry in disbelief.

'It's a long story … but there was an engagement at a place called Kafr Dowar. The King's men were doing some reconnaissance and came under fire. An officer was down, badly wounded, and a Private Garvey asked permission to stay with him … he did so, binding wounds … very brave man. He was from Bradford, in Yorkshire. This particular man served in India, and was wounded there … and then in Egypt against that swine Arabi … a soldier turned rebel he was.'

Harry was intrigued.

'There is more. Garvey was awarded the Victoria Cross. As you know, the words 'For Valour' are on that very distinguished item. Two words … over yet another kind of flower I suppose.'

Harry gave a gasp of astonishment. 'Are you saying that our hired killer is a hero of the Empire, Colonel?'

'It's possible. There were only seven Yorkshiremen in the list I compiled. I know we were applying merely educated guesswork, but still …'

'Then we may have the name of our man … but damn it, Colonel, we still don't know where he lives, if he lives anywhere at all. He may be one of those thousands who crawl from lodging house to lodging house … we're no further on with this, and I need to move fast, Colonel.'

Harry thanked Colonel Ranger and was out in the street in seconds, on his way to meet Eddie. They may have a name, but it was one attached to an action of the utmost courage, not infamy.

———

Jack Garvey had made his drunken way to Covent Garden and was asking passers-by for directions to Bedford Street. Under the rough exterior, he was still in possession of that code of honour he had always lived by. If someone paid you to do a job, then you did it. If an officer gave you an order, you obeyed him. It might be a fallen world, but a man could still do right. Many times before he had walked these streets, seeing a landscape of poor, benighted souls, abandoned by those with the power. These corrupt men in fine suits, like this solicitor, they had to be weeded out.

They tried to kill me in India, Sir. Came at me from behind. But them Ghurkas saved me … fine men them Ghurkas, Sir. But let me stay with him, this man is bleeding and he needs me …

His head spun. He felt that he needed to rest, to sit down somewhere. Sachs could wait. Gaggles of city folk came past, smirking and ridiculing, higher-than-thou gents, young bloods ready to flutter away fortunes, or pick a fight with any stray, homeless drifting piece of human flotsam. No, he had to rest for a minute. Then a sign cleared in his view. There were the words The White Lion, a supper club. Yes, he knew right away that Molly McCardle would be there, and she would sing that song just for him. He started to sing it, *'My heart began to fly ... and I'm so happy I could cry ...'* The Lord's best gift to frail humanity was a good drink, and Molly would be there too. He took some steps towards the door and was soon inside, on the edge of a crowd. He laid an arm across the back of a fat man in front, then applied some pressure. There was a cry as the man fell forward.

'Hey! Who are you pushing?'

'I wanna see Molly ... she's singing, I can hear her singing.' Garvey forced his way through the crowd towards a large back room where there were broad tables, people seated, and on a low stage that ran along the length of the room, there was Molly McCardle. She was sitting on a swing, the ropes covered with paper roses, wound around. From her arm there hung a lace-topped reticule and on her head a little girl's folded hat with a band around it.

He sat at a long table, again pushing in. A man grabbed hold of his collar and then, seeing his ribboned chest exclaimed, 'My Gawd ... a Victoria Cross!'

Jack looked up at Molly and called out her name. She swung gently on the flowery swing and came to a stop as her song ended. There was loud applause and a host of cat-calls and whistles. Then she heard one voice calling to her: 'Molly ... Molly my dear, sing "My Heart Began to Fly".'

She knew the voice. Standing up and stepping forward, a smile to melt the toughest heart, she said, 'One of my regulars hey! I hear you, mister, I hear you. Here's a song requested by this Tommy ... he's got a VC on his chest and love in his heart, folks!'

From the far door, Harry, who had been keeping watch on the pub for three days, heard her words. He had Leo with him; it was too exposed a place to be on your own, and Leo had offered. They knew at once that they had their man. Harry's first response was to rush the crowd and get to the man, but he soon realised that Garvey would not be going anywhere until Molly finished the song. He dashed out into the street to find any constables who might be around. Of course, Harry knew that Jack had not broken the law – he had not hurt anyone and had been nowhere near Sachs – but they had to stop him before he did. Leo was moving in his wake, but Harry called, 'Stay there, in case he runs!'

Molly McCardle was stepping this way and that, in a little dance, entrancing the crowd with *'All he did was kiss me, but my heart began to fly'*. She cupped a hand to one ear, encouraging them to sing along, and the crowd responded, well trained. The loudest voice belonged to Jack Garvey and he boomed out the last verse,

'I'm so happy I could cry,
And I don't want to wonder why,
There's a warm tear in my eye,
And all that he did was to kiss me ...'

Jack tried to scramble up onto the stage, and as Molly stepped back, Leo and two burly men came from the side, towards him. He saw them and rushed instead towards the back door, blowing a last kiss to Molly, who blew a kiss back to him.

He was soon out in the cold air, sweat running down his face and his heart beating so powerfully that it thumped in his throat. For some time he closed his eyes and all he could see was Molly McCardle's face. *I never had no chance of a good woman ... never had a chance, Captain!*

His breathing gradually slowed and he felt for the bayonet, still held firmly inside his coat in a deep pocket, in its metal case. Touching it brought back his sense of duty, and he reminded himself what he must do. The night was closing in now. Not far away, he heard a whistle blow and voices were calling out his name. 'This is the police, Jack Garvey ... give yourself up!'

He knew where he was going now – just two corners away was the man he had to see out of the world. Yes, this Sachs, who was threatening a good man. He turned towards his destination, driven by the kind of instinct that guides a hunter to his prey.

Eddie and a detective sergeant strode from inn to inn, questioning the loafers and the drifters. From a throng of drunks singing an old ballad, a constable came towards them. 'No use, Guv. This Tommy … not a soul seems to know him, or if they do, they're keeping quiet about it.'

'Right, give it up for tonight constable, get the men back to the station. We've wasted enough time on this,' Eddie said. It was the constable who first heard Harry shouting for assistance. When they met, Harry explained that Jack Garvey was inside the supper club and they rushed back, hoping to find their man still admiring the singer, but the bird had flown, and Harry joined the police and Eddie for a trawl of the surrounding streets.

'We're near Sachs's office … he's got to be going there,' Eddie said. 'Harry, we'll head straight there – sergeant, gather the two armed detectives and follow us … fourteen Bedford Street!'

Harry and Eddie moved as quickly as they could, but Harry could not keep up. 'Damn, I'm too old for this, Carney!' He had to stop and recover his breath. 'We must press on Harry,' urged Eddie, 'it's a matter of life and death!'

At the corner of St Paul's Eddie called out, 'Just around here … down Henrietta Street and there we are – come on!' He was very much the younger and fitter man and he pushed on. At the end of

Henrietta Street he looked right and he could hear a banging. He ran toward the sound, calling out behind, telling Harry to turn right.

Jack had kicked his way into the solicitor's office. The door gave way to the sheer brutality of his attack, and as he stood in the room, there was Sachs, sitting at the desk. But as he saw the man before him, he yelled out, 'Detective come!' Sergeant Davis was shaving in the back room, but he ran in. His coat was over a chair, his gun in the pocket, and he dived for it, but Jack got to him first and swung his fist at the officer's jaw, sending him onto the floor. Sachs jumped up and ran towards the back of the room in fear.

'You must be the bag o' bones I'm after – Mr Sachs, right? Well, I got this for you.' Jack took out the bayonet from the case and held it high, moving forward and lunging at Sachs, who stood against the wall, paralysed with terror.

At that second a crack snapped out from the doorway and a bullet slammed into the soldier's back, sending him crashing forward against the desk. He fell to the ground, rolling onto his side, and then onto his back. The bayonet fell away, clattering to the floor.

Davis had staggered back to his feet and Eddie Carney moved forward, still holding the pistol. They stood over the dying man, who had one hand over his chest, clutching the Victoria Cross. His head rocked as he said, 'Nearly made it, Sir. Too many of the enemy … cowards came from behind me!' He froze in death, his eyes like glass in a waxwork.

'We killed a very dangerous man, Davis,' said Eddie. Harry, who had now arrived, still fighting for breath, said, 'Yes, but you also killed a very courageous man, one who loved his country,' and he saluted the dead man.

'We helped the Honourable Sir John Tardow, future Member of Parliament, Harry. But this was another honourable man – gone wrong.'

'Indeed, and if I am not mistaken, had this killing taken place, Mr Tardow would be heading for some penal servitude in a convict prison.'

Eddie nodded. 'Yes. In fact, I think we're looking down at the honourable man.'

———

Molly McCardle had retreated from the stage and was in her makeshift dressing room, where Leo had used his charm to gain entrance. He looked every inch the aristocrat, and Molly was familiar with his type.

'They let you in then ... my strong-arms?'

'Oh yes ... but rest assured I'm here for entirely honourable purposes. I'm protecting you from that obnoxious man who was at the front of the crowd out there.'

'I've got some very capable protectors thank you, Mr ... ' She looked him up and down and decided that he would have money to spend on her.

'Aubrey Leo Antoine at your service!' He tipped his head, taking off his brown bowler as he did so.

'What? Not *the* Aubrey Antoine, the novelist?'

'Yes, I am he. Would you care for dinner, my dear?'

She smiled and told him to wait while she took off her stage clothes. 'Turn away, there's a nice gentleman!'

Leo helped himself to a glass of brandy on her table and thought that, just for a change, when the next case came up he would insist on being the detective, with Harry as his assistant. On the other hand, he thought, as he caught a glimpse of a lovely ankle, there were compensations ...

———

Sachs never learnt what Tardow had done. The story he heard was that a madman on the loose had been tracked down and stopped. But the libel case had to go on, and Floriana Dalia was told that she was Meg Caley of Spitalfields. She tried very hard to deny it, but she lived in a world in which fallen women stayed down in the dark where no one could be shamed by them, or so the press said.

One day, as the trial was in full flow, John Tardow came down to breakfast and was told that his wife had gone, her destination unknown and no letter of explanation left for her husband. He never stood for Parliament and spent most of his time and attention growing vegetables and dreaming of Paris.

About the Author

Stephen Wade teaches creative writing part-time at the University of Hull. He is also a freelance writer and historian who specialises in crime and military history. He regularly writes for local and family history magazines and is involved with running oral history workshops. His previous non-fiction titles include *Lincolnshire Murders*, *Hanged at Lincoln* and *The A-Z of Curious Lincolnshire*. This is his first fiction title. He lives in Scunthorpe, Lincolnshire.

Visit our website and discover thousands of other History Press books.

www.thehistorypress.co.uk

Lightning Source UK Ltd.
Milton Keynes UK
UKOW03f1249120814

236818UK00001B/1/P